MAVERICK'S LADY

Linda Jenkins

A KISMET™ Romance

METEOR PUBLISHING CORPORATION
Bensalem, Pennsylvania

To Linda Wright.

Because she's always believed that
Reid was special.

LINDA JENKINS

A native Missourian, Linda Jenkins calls herself a "naturalized" Texan, having lived in Houston off and on for almost fifteen years. She likes strong women, stronger men and anyone who can make her laugh. In addition to her writing career, she and her husband are business partners, and they share a house with the three cats who have so generously adopted them.

ONE

"Honey, I'll warn you up front. I eat little girls for breakfast."

Bentley North kept her face impassive for a few seconds while she studied the well-dressed desperado across the desk from her. *Now* that's *an original way to begin a job interview*! His threat surprised her, made her curious about his need to issue it. More than anything, it amused her. She didn't allow herself to laugh.

Instead, she smiled and looked directly at him, then had to glance away momentarily. No way did she believe a man with such warm, hazel-flecked brown eyes ate little girls for breakfast. But she responded as though she took his warning seriously. "I don't doubt it, Mr. Hunter. However, you might find a grown-up woman like me hard to digest." She spoke in the confident, even-timbred voice that had served her so well in the courtrooms of Manhattan.

His lazy-lidded eyes narrowed even more and he scrutinized her for a long minute. Bentley tempered the smile and endured his silent appraisal, matching the intensity of his gaze. Reid Hunter didn't strike her as the type to appreciate her small put-down, even if he deserved it.

Actually, he deserved worse. She had arrived on time for the interview, then waited thirty minutes in the reception area, plus an additional half hour in his office. Exasperated by his rudeness, she had been about to walk out when he charged in through a side door.

Bentley had sat up straighter, alert because the room had suddenly come alive with dynamic energy. He offered no explanation for his lateness, nor did he bother with a greeting or introduction. Just took possession of his chair and tossed out that absurd warning.

She had felt compelled to retaliate.

When his reaction finally came, it startled her. He threw back his head and laughed, a lusty sound that rolled up from his chest and escaped through parted lips. The laugh was contagious, the kind that made her want to join in. Bentley decided against it. She wasn't sure if he was laughing at the cleverness of her remark or at her foolhardiness for making it.

"Touché," he said, and leaned forward to plant his forearms on the desk. His eyes still pinning her, he rapped her resume with his knuckles. "So, you think I should give you a job. Tell me some of your attributes."

She shouldn't say it. She couldn't help herself. "I'm punctual."

His thumb and forefinger stroked a full, dark mustache and one eyebrow climbed. "Trying to score points, North? I've already allowed you one."

"Something tells me I'm going to need all I can get." Her calm voice belied a growing uneasiness. No matter how confidently she spoke, this wasn't going at all as she'd anticipated. Bentley had experienced a

rush of awareness—no, wariness was more accurate—
the instant she saw him. She ought to have paid more
attention to it.

He appeared to relax as he lounged against the high
back of his leather chair, but she sensed the pose was
deceptive. "Then you'd better know I give up few
points and never the game."

His tone dared her to defy him; his voice reverberated
like distant, rumbling thunder, jolting her with its visceral effect. She felt the vibrations clearly, powerfully,
as if she'd touched their source. More than what he
said, his low flinty resonance ate away at her poise.
Instinct told her he aimed to best her in their verbal
skirmish and that she'd be wise to retreat enough to
ensure his win.

"Game, set, and match, Mr. Hunter," she said with
as much deference as she could muster. "Now shall
we discuss the position? You have it. I want it."

Those few minutes at the desk seemed to exhaust his
ability to sit still. He stood abruptly and stalked to the
window where he stared out over the rambling Houston
headquarters of his company, Maverick Enterprises.
Bentley assumed the delay was another intimidation tactic and bit back the urge to tell him it wouldn't work.
She'd swum with a few sharks in her time; too many
to fall prey to one so obvious as Reid Hunter.

Looking up at him she had to concede that if he
chose, he probably could intimidate most people. Renegade Reid, the media's favorite term for him, was a
nickname he'd clearly earned. His daring business ex-
ploits, combined with one of the most abrasive person-
alities she'd ever encountered, made him a formidable
figure. And at least six feet three inches of sinewy lean-

ness gave him the added advantage of looking down on nearly everyone.

But Bentley's overriding impression of him was one of unrelenting toughness. She could easily picture him a hundred years ago, stalking his quarry with a Colt revolver strapped to his hip.

Backlit by a sunny window, she saw underlying glints of mahogany when he ran both hands through his dark-brown hair. Like the rest of him, it looked barely tamed, as if he never took time to do more than comb it with his fingers. It grew over his ears, and the ends curled in stark contrast against his white collar.

She watched him pace to a small, concealed refrigerator in the corner and rearrange its contents until he found a pitcher of orange juice. He gestured an offer to her, but she shook her head, wishing he'd alight long enough to finish the interview.

"Mr. Hunter, about the job—"

"I don't think you're the right person for it," he announced calmly, watching her as he chunked ice into a glass. When he saw her bristle, then recover, a sly smile played with the corners of his mouth. "No, in fact I'm sure you're all wrong for Maverick."

"If you've read my resume—"

"I have."

"Surely you aren't suggesting that I don't have the right credentials." Bentley wondered if she'd scored a point for finishing a sentence.

"Your credentials are most impressive, Ms. North. Snobby schools, snobby downtown law firm—"

"Prosecutor's office, southern district of Manhattan," she added, seizing the opportunity to interrupt him.

"Yes, but the head of my legal department tells me

that's exactly the right thing for an up-and-coming attorney to do." He shook his head as he drained the glass. "I think we'll both be better off if you head back downtown."

For a fleeting second, Bentley almost obeyed the impulse to say what *she* thought. Which definitely would not earn points. She'd interviewed for only three jobs in her life and had gotten them all. Unaccustomed to failure, she didn't relish the prospect of it now.

Sensing it was vital to maintain self-assurance with this man, she summoned her most convincing courtroom voice. "Would you explain why you think I won't fit into your company?"

He went to refill his glass, this time with milk, then came around the desk and leaned against the edge, long legs extended toward her. Up close he looked even more substantial and more than a little menacing. Bentley experienced a pang of uncertainty, felt it settle in her stomach, told herself to ignore it.

"Seems obvious to me why you won't fit in. I like to hire people who've struggled to get where they are, people who aren't afraid to jump in and fight when it's necessary." He gave her a piercing look and drawled, "You, Ms. North, don't impress me as someone who's had to work very hard for anything you have."

She found it more and more difficult to restrain her temper in the face of his persistent needling. Her head throbbed and one hand curled into a fist. She never allowed anyone to provoke her into losing control, but Reid Hunter was coming close, and even more maddening, she was sure he knew it. "Hide and watch if you think I don't know how to fight. You might learn a thing or two."

"Why do you want to work for my company?"

Keeping the opposition off balance was good strategy, a tactic she often used herself. "I practiced corporate law for a year and found it tedious and boring. During the next two, I was involved in some low-down prosecution work, and while that's very interesting, it tends to get depressing."

She didn't add that it could also be dangerous, so much so that it had finally driven her to leave New York. Bentley suppressed a shudder of dread and forged ahead. "Now I'm looking for a challenge, fascinating work that, at the same time, will be fun."

"Fun!" Hunter slammed the glass to his desk, sloshing milk on the polished cherry surface. He ignored the spill. "You expect your work to be fun?"

"Why not? If you don't enjoy your job, you've got the wrong one."

He didn't comment on that, but she thought a genuine smile hid beneath the mustache. "I'll make a decision in the next two weeks. You will be considered along with the other applicants." He stood and walked around his desk.

Bentley couldn't accept his casual dismissal. "Mr. Hunter, I know you aren't convinced, but *I am* right for this job." She rose to face him, drawing her five feet eight inches into a regal pose. "I can do it better than anyone else. Hire me and I'll prove it."

Without waiting for a reply, she walked to the door and opened it. Then she turned and gave him her most dazzling smile. "I'll expect to hear from you." The door clicked shut behind her with precisely the right amount of force.

Reid dropped into the chair and propped his feet, ankles crossed, on the desk. "Oh, yeah. Count on it." He chuckled. She didn't know it yet, but she had the job. He didn't even plan to talk to anyone else. She'd guaranteed herself the position by saying she wanted her work to be fun. That echoed his own attitude, making other differences insignificant. It was the one trait he demanded of his employees.

He stabbed the intercom to his secretary. "Cancel the rest of those interviews for legal, Mrs. T."

He heard her smile when she spoke. "Hired her on the spot, did you?"

"You know me better than that."

"I guess you realize she's not overly impressed with the notorious Reid Hunter," the matronly voice shot back, sounding delighted by that news.

He chuckled again. "She will be. Just needs some time to appreciate my endearing qualities."

"You'll have to get some first. Even then, I wouldn't take any bets. That one's got class. What does she need with a maverick like you?"

Marian Tolliver had been the first employee Reid hired for his fledgling company eight years ago. Right away, he'd learned she was honest to the point of being downright blunt. But she was also loyal and efficient, and his ego was secure enough to withstand her good-natured attacks.

"Notify personnel about our newest employee," he said, cutting her off. After dashing a notation on the desk calendar, he threaded his hands behind his head and tilted the chair back.

"Damn!" What had possessed him to come on like a macho bully? Reid was nobody's patsy, but he couldn't recall ever acting quite that way. He'd admit he wasn't much of a sweet-talker where women were concerned. Still, he managed to treat them with a gruff sort of gallantry that they seemed to find acceptable.

From the moment he saw Bentley North sitting there, regal as Queen Victoria, he'd been compelled to establish his dominance, show her that he was in control of their relationship.

Relationship? Where had that come from? She was just looking for a job. Because *the Wall Street Journal* had called Maverick one of the fastest growing, most progressive-thinking corporations in the country, personnel was deluged with applications. North was no different from hundreds of others.

"Sure, sure." As if every woman he interviewed had honeyed skin and dove-gray eyes that could either assess him with cool disdain or flash with fire. And that mouth . . . Even when she'd briefly lost her cool and glared at him, her lips had been parted. Inviting. He had wanted—been tempted—to help himself to a taste.

Reid jumped to his feet as an uncomfortable sensation swept over him. "Good Lord!" It was crazy to sit here daydreaming about how perfectly they'd fit together in other ways. He had an iron-clad rule about keeping his private life, such as it was, separate from business.

With Bentley, he could either mount a full-scale pursuit or he could hire her, but not both. Scowling, he loosened his tie. Never one for self-delusion, Reid knew he was going to break his rule and damn the consequences. Why?

The answer was so simple it shocked him. He'd never met a woman like this before. "Well, Hunter, you didn't get where you are without taking chances." He rubbed his hands together in anticipation. "This will be a sweetheart of a fight, North, and guess who's going to come out on top?"

* * *

Bentley dug for her sunglasses the minute she stepped out and was slapped by a wave of heat and humidity, both in the midnineties. Since she'd returned to her hometown three days ago, she had often asked herself why anyone in his right mind would move here now, when summer loomed like a damp, suffocating specter.

"You'd think he could put everyone in a single building," she complained as she retraced the convoluted route back to the main reception area where she'd parked.

Maverick headquarters filled six buildings, and the whole complex looked like an aging hacienda that had spawned mutant offspring of varying sizes and shapes, then cast them off at odd angles to the main structure. Some were connected by bougainvillea-covered arbors, others by brick-paved walks. The only common elements were buff-colored stucco exteriors, red tiled roofs, and lush landscaping. The overall effect was attractive in an eccentric kind of way, and probably said a lot about Reid Hunter.

By the time she reached her mother's sedate Oldsmobile, Bentley's pink-and-gray patterned silk dress clung to her as limply as if she had plunged into the fountain she'd just passed in the courtyard. She switched the air conditioner to full blast and directed all the vents toward her.

A glance at the dashboard clock made her grimace. "Curse the man!" She had boasted to Mr. Hunter about her punctuality; now she was late for a lunch date downtown. Smiling, she turned onto Allen Parkway. It wouldn't matter if she showed up four hours late. Bill Rutledge wouldn't complain. Bentley was one of the few people her stepfather never lost patience with.

Ten minutes later she turned the car over to valet parking and rode an elevator to the Petroleum Club atop an oil company building.

"B.B.! Over here!" boomed an unmistakable East Texas voice. Bentley waved and joined a cluster of men. After she greeted familiar faces and met several new members, Bill steered her to his favorite table.

He frowned at her while chomping on his ever-present unlit cigar. "You look like you've been tied to a whippin' post, B.B."

"Such flattery. Count on you for a dose of reality."

He snorted. "I warned you. That boy's a barracuda. Have to be to get where he is at his age."

Wild Bill Rutledge looked as if he'd just stepped off an oil rig, and he had never lost the pronounced twang of his native area. But anyone who underestimated him usually regretted it. He had combined hard work and tenacity to parlay a few leases into a successful independent oil company. Lots of people had done that in the boom years. Surviving the bust had been even trickier.

"What happened?" he demanded, toying with a gold matchbook, as if he planned to light the forbidden cigar.

Bentley knew she'd never fool him by glossing over this morning's fiasco. Before she began, she took a sip of the wine Bill had ordered for her. "Honestly, you can't imagine that interview. He doesn't even believe in basic courtesies." She related the details of their meeting. "What nerve! Telling me to go back to that snobby—his word—downtown law firm." This time she didn't bother hiding the anger she'd suppressed earlier. "I was tempted to tell him exactly what to do with his job."

Bill guffawed and whacked the table hard enough to jingle the silverware. "That's my girl. So did you get up and walk out?" He sounded hopeful.

"I can't explain why, but I'd swear that's not his normal behavior. I read an article that said Maverick has an unusually high ratio of female executives, so I can't figure out why he took that sexist attitude with me."

Bentley looked out over Houston's space-age skyline, remembering their battle of words. "In a way, I enjoyed it. And while I got in the last word literally, I think the symbolic victory goes to him."

Bill observed her closely, searching for what she'd left unsaid. At last he shook his head, as if the conclusion was hard to fathom. "You admire him."

"Of course. A good attorney always respects a worthy adversary. But interesting as it was, I'm not going to get the job." A job she had wanted. Badly. "Now I'm back to square one, just another unemployment statistic."

"I'm glad. Never did understand why you wanted to work for Maverick when I've had an office ready for you since your law school graduation." He gave Bentley an adoring look. "You've known all along that I expect you to take over my job at Willco. What do you say? Won't be a better time than right now."

She pointed an accusing finger and tried to divert him. "Bill, you know you're not ready to step down. You'll still be running things twenty years from now."

"Hell, girl! At my age I don't even buy a green banana." He laughed with her, but didn't drop the subject. "I'd like to see you settled in the company, especially now." His eyes shifted away from Bentley, unfocused.

"Bill, is anything wrong at Willco? A problem or—" She grasped his arm and forced him to look at her. "You're not ill, are you?" she demanded, numb with dread.

"Aw, darlin', you know how unstable the oil business has been, up and down for years now." He tossed the cigar into an ashtray. "More down than up, it seems."

"Are you in some kind of financial bind?"

"No, no," he reassured her. "We're not getting fat, as you know from your dividends. But the debt picture is still good and management has always worked lean."

"But something's bothering you. I can tell."

Bill touched his stomach. "It's not a problem I can put my finger on. More like a gut feeling that something's going on." He sat in silence for a time. "Maybe my instincts are playing tricks on me in my old age. Or maybe I'm just trying to persuade you to help me out. Think of the fun we can have running Willco together."

"You scoundrel." She gave him an affectionate pat on the arm. "You have plenty of fun without me." She stopped his interruption with a promise. "When the time comes that you really need me, I'll be there."

Bill had begun talking about Bentley succeeding him ever since he'd married her widowed mother fourteen years earlier. She'd never had the heart to tell him that managing an oil company didn't interest her.

Law and its myriad applications were what fascinated Bentley. She wanted to apply her skills within the framework of a large corporate operation . . . like Maverick. A person could learn so much from a master like Reid Hunter. But since she rarely agonized over what might have been, she grinned and pointed at a neighboring table. "Do you intend to feed me or shall I snitch that salmon fillet from Weldon Gray's plate?"

Bill threw up his hands in surrender, then summoned a waiter. And when they finished eating, he drove her to where his surprise welcome-home gift awaited. "It's all yours," he said, opening the door of a luxurious sports car.

Bentley's eyes widened. "Bill, this is far too extravagant!" she exclaimed as she peered through the open sun roof.

" 'Course it's not. When I was your age, I couldn't afford a machine like this. Now I'm too bulky and stove-up to get in it. So indulge me 'cause I want you to have it."

"You're the one who's indulging me," she said, giving him an enthusiastic hug. "And I love you for it." She kissed his cheek and, unable to curb her excitement any longer, dove into the soft tan leather seat. She gripped the wheel and let the new car smell envelop her. "It's beautiful, Bill. Thank you."

"My pleasure." He closed the door, its heavy thunk attesting to the vehicle's solidity. "Go on, hon. Give 'er a try."

Minutes later as Bentley sped down Woodway, she tossed her head back and laughed aloud. She had wanted the Maverick job, but this was one fine consolation prize. The sleek Jaguar XJS behaved much like its jungle namesake. Held in check, it purred nicely. Unleashed, it had more power than she'd ever need.

She got on the Loop, but at three o'clock, early rush hour traffic already clogged every lane. Taking the first exit, she started back to her family's River Oaks house. One more day and she could move into her nearby townhouse and begin the process of getting settled.

Now that meant more job interviews, a possibility she hadn't considered before this morning when Reid Hunter had taught her that the line between self-confidence and conceit is very narrow.

No need to dwell on it. As Bill had advised her at lunch, worry is like a rocking chair. It gives you something to do, but it never gets you anywhere.

When she arrived at the white brick colonial, Victoria Rutledge invited Bentley to join her and Bill for dinner with a group of their friends. But Bentley didn't feel in a sociable mood. She decided instead to raid the refrigerator and watch a tape of her favorite old movie.

Lying in bed later that evening, she put the disastrous clash with Hunter in perspective. Maverick was, after all, his company, and he had a right to employ whomever he chose. His wasn't the only job in town. Houston was back, teeming with raw vitality and its famed wide-open approach to doing business. She could find a place in the midst of all the movers and shakers.

But first, maybe what she needed was some winding-down time. She hadn't taken a vacation in close to two years, and her previous job had been fraught with tension, especially that final case. Bentley shivered and clamped the pillow over her ears, trying to block out the sinister voice that had turned her phone into an implement of terror. Those harrowing threats had finally become so frequent and explicit, her office had insisted she have protection. Every step she'd taken during the last two weeks in New York had been with an escort at her side.

Even that hadn't thwarted her tormentor.

In frustrated rage, she hurled her pillow across the room. The horror was behind her. She'd come home—

to be safe again, to start over. There was so much to look forward to.

Like her law school roommate's wedding. She turned on her side and studied the yellow dress that had been delivered that afternoon. Imagine an avowed career woman like Lenore getting married, to a Greek tycoon, no less.

The image of another tycoon appeared unbidden. She recalled her initial impression of Reid Hunter as a gun-slinging desperado. She hadn't known then just how accurate that assessment would prove. Or how ruth-lessly he would shoot her down.

Everything he had said drifted around inside her head. Why did he think she'd never worked hard? If anything, the opposite held true. Bentley was smart, but not brilliant enough to excel in her studies and her work without effort. At least she had set him straight about her ability to fight. She'd take him on in a minute.

A scene of her taking him on flashed through her consciousness in vivid detail. Only they weren't fight-ing. "Damn you! Leave me alone."

To her disgust, she had to repeat the same command every night for the next several weeks. Images of him followed her everywhere. Every time she shut her eyes that dark nemesis was there to haunt her. And when she returned to Houston from Lenore's wedding and a vacation in Greece, his secretary had left messages every day.

Reid glanced at the well-worn resume, then at his watch. Five minutes to wait, if she was as punctual as she'd informed him with a mixture of humor and haughtiness that annoyed him almost as much as it intrigued him.

Bentley Brighton North. Such a stodgy name. He wondered what her family and friends called her. Her lovers. Reid swore eloquently, the colorful words interrupted by Marian's announcement of the lady's arrival.

"Send her in, Mrs. T." He stood, determined that their second interview would go more smoothly than the first. His secretary opened the door to admit Bentley, tanned and smiling. He swallowed and wished she dressed for success. Silk dresses swirling around her long legs made him want . . . He smiled, too.

"Ms. North. Thank you for coming back. Sit down." He indicated a grouping of wing chairs and a sofa in one corner. "Would you like anything to drink?"

Bentley sat on the edge of one of the chairs. "No, nothing for me." She hoped she'd managed to disguise her amusement at his strained politeness. She suspected he rarely bothered to play the gracious host.

He popped the top on a caffeine-free cola, sank onto the sofa, and drained half the can. "I assume you're familiar with the scope of Maverick Enterprises." At her nod, he said, "If you were in my place, what direction would you take a corporation like this for, say, the next ten years?"

Bentley thought the question might better be posed to financial planners, but she gave him a detailed answer based on her research of business trends. His expression remained emotionless. She couldn't tell if he agreed or not.

"If I told you I'm interested in acquiring an oil company, how would you advise me to go about it?"

Though she knew a great deal about the subject, an

odd sensation flitted down her spine. She disregarded it and described in great detail the possible options. He seemed impressed.

Bentley began to feel optimistic. He was going to offer her the position. She could sense it. Confidence bubbled up from inside her and burst forth in an expectant smile. She was envisioning a champagne celebration tonight.

"Well, North, I think you're probably capable of handling the job. The question is, how far will you go to get it?"

TWO

Don't react. Bentley willed herself to swallow the anger, to betray none of the volatile emotions that roiled inside her. An all-too-familiar sensation of being captive in a situation she couldn't control swamped her. But she refused to knuckle under this time. Reid Hunter was not a mobster. She could handle him.

When she was certain she had her temper under control, she answered his question as if it were perfectly reasonable. "I'll follow orders. I will work as many hours as necessary, including nights and weekends, and I'm free to travel."

Pleased at how equable her voice sounded, she decided to risk a small barb of her own. "I'm even willing to accept the salary, although I think you're somewhat low in that area."

He crossed his arms and stared at her, steely-eyed. "Mmm, but you're not showing me any extraordinary motivation. Anyone who wants the job would do as much. I'm looking for that . . . *extra* something."

If a pause could be suggestive, his was. Bentley

closed her eyes briefly and expelled a surreptitious breath. She felt like asking him why he was bothering with this rehash of their first interview. Instead she opted to play the scene to its end and happily see the last of Mr. Hunter.

"If the job has other requirements, you'll have to spell them out for me."

"I'm sure you've read the description. That says it all." His fingers drummed a restless cadence against his thigh, but his eyes remained fixed on her. "I'm just trying to get a feel for how ambitious you are."

"Then let me tell you. I'm *very* ambitious and I intend to come out on top. But I don't plan any horizontal moves, if that's what you had in mind."

"How disappointing." His smile was sly, his nod too satisfied. "Here I was thinking you might have designs on me."

Words like arrogant, conceited, and egotistical warred inside her head. She ached to puncture his smugness. It was ridiculous to sit here and let him goad her further, but her competitive nature wouldn't allow her to back down. "I might have designs on your office. Never on you."

He laughed, much as he had on that first day. "Your file says you can start in three weeks. Make it one and you're hired."

Stunned, Bentley rose and looked down at him. She heard herself speak before thinking about what she intended to say. "Split the difference and I'll work extra hard my first week."

"Done. Eight o'clock, two weeks from today." He stood, too, extending his hand.

She shook it, a quick, businesslike exchange, but her initial reaction to him came back with a rush. He radiated such a pervasive energy that their brief connection had been akin to touching a power source. She reached the door before he spoke again.

"One last thing, North. Don't forget you're on trial. I'll be watching you very closely."

She went with his choice of words. "As you know, I have a successful trial record."

"Yeah, but you'll find I'm a hard-nosed judge, maybe the toughest you'll ever encounter."

"I've never met one I couldn't work with," she said, sneaking in the last word before she closed the door on his sardonic grin.

Bentley slumped against the dark panel and drew a couple of restorative breaths. In those few minutes, Reid Hunter had elicited a dizzying range of feelings. She'd done her best to subdue them, but she couldn't deny that the man disturbed her. His first words to her might not have been an idle threat after all. He probably did eat little girls for breakfast.

"Oh, dear." The kind voice interrupted her reverie. Marian Tolliver looked at Bentley with what appeared to be a mixture of understanding and sympathy. Then she smiled, deepening a network of small creases that framed her bright-blue eyes. "I try to avoid clichés like the plague, but in this case I think one is appropriate. His bark *is* worse than his bite."

Bentley managed a short laugh. "I think I can keep up with him, if I train for it. You know, sharpen my tongue, toughen my hide, that sort of thing."

Mrs. T. giggled, an unexpected sound from someone her age. "That might not be a bad idea. But I meant what I said. Reid's a darling boy. Once you've proven yourself, you will find him a pleasure to work for."

Bentley moved to stand in front of the older woman's

desk, thinking of all the ways she might describe her new employer. "Darling boy" did not make the list. "I suppose the casualty rate for those of us trying to prove ourselves is staggering."

Marian looked astounded. "Why, not at all. Reid has an incredible talent for picking the right people. That's why he personally interviews every applicant above a certain level. Turnover at Maverick is very low." Her periwinkle-blue eyes locked with Bentley's. "He seldom makes a mistake."

On the drive home, Bentley reflected on Mrs. Tolliver's statement. Reid Hunter's mistakes might be rare; she only hoped she hadn't just made the biggest one of her life by accepting his job offer.

She frowned, impatient with the vacillation. All her life she'd been confident and decisive, in charge of her own fate. One hand closed in a fist on the steering wheel as she battled the recurring helplessness. Never again would she allow any man to control her emotions, be he good or evil.

By the time she pulled into her garage, she had convinced herself that matching wits with Hunter would be a challenging contest. She could have started work right away, but had demanded the two weeks on principle. With a man like that, one took any slight advantage one could get.

Bentley spent her days getting settled in the small group of townhouses on the edge of the River Oaks shopping area. Close to where she'd grown up, it had the added bonus of being within a few minutes' drive of her new job. Evenings she saw old friends and caught up on what had been going on during the two years she'd spent in New York.

Her mother filled the house with relatives to celebrate Bentley's homecoming, and Bill acted so much like his usual sunny self that they almost forgot his recent preoccupation with business.

But no matter how busy Bentley was, Reid Hunter hovered around the edges of her awareness, waiting to dominate her thoughts. In the quiet time alone, she found herself increasingly willing to give him the attention he demanded. And she anticipated her first day at Maverick with equal parts of exhilaration and apprehension.

When Paul Westlake called to invite her to the company's picnic, Bentley accepted. Paul was a childhood friend and law school classmate at the University of Virginia. They'd stayed in touch, and when he heard about the opening in the legal department at Maverick, Paul had contacted her.

The festivities were in full swing when they arrived at the large pavilion in Bear Creek Park around four in the afternoon. One of the first things Bentley saw was a dark shaggy head looming above the crowd. Wearing jeans that had been laundered to near-oblivion and a similarly aged Purdue jersey, Reid presided over several iced kegs of beer.

He pumped the foamy liquid into black mugs which had a silver Maverick logo imprinted on the side. She wasn't a very dedicated beer drinker, but Bentley soon found a mug thrust into her hands. She turned slightly and faced her new boss, who looked down at her with that infuriating sly grin he had perfected so well.

His gaze transferred to her escort before resting again on her. "You sure don't waste any time, Westlake. North hasn't even started work and you've already made a move."

"Paul and I are old friends, Mr. Hunter. We go back a long way." It annoyed her to be on the defensive so soon.

His brows arched and he chuckled. "I'll bet."

She refused to even think about what that mocking remark meant. She hadn't come prepared to do battle, didn't feel up to it. "If you'll excuse me, I think I'll circulate. Looks like there are lots of people to meet."

Reid plunked an empty mug into Paul's hand, relegating the younger man to bartending, while he took Bentley's arm and steered her toward a group at one of the tables. She longed to shake free of his firm grip, but suspected he'd only make an issue of it. Scenes were his specialty. "I'll come willingly, Mr. Hunter. After all, it wouldn't be judicious to run from the boss."

"You'll run plenty until I close in," he muttered cryptically. Before she could dispute that, he stopped to introduce her to Jim Lawson, head of Maverick's legal department. Bentley liked him on sight, mainly because any man who'd show up at a company function wearing a fuchsia Hawaiian shirt and lime-green walking shorts had to have a sense of humor.

Reid continued to show her off, like a prized heifer he'd acquired to improve his herd, she mused. How paradoxical that he paid her lavish compliments in front of others, when he'd gone out of his way to irritate her at their two previous meetings. Oh, well, figuring out his modus operandi wasn't necessary. She was going to work for him, not put him on the witness stand.

The crowd grew steadily throughout the afternoon. Bentley tried to keep track of all the faces and names, knowing it was impossible. Reid was never far away and she felt his eyes on her almost constantly. His attention was unsettling and she wanted to discount it. She couldn't, because it was also exciting.

A boisterous volleyball game had been in progress for several hours, the participants shuttling in and out. Bentley thrived on competition so she joined in, giving and receiving her share of cheers and hoots. A duel developed at the net between her and an athletic-looking man from the marketing department.

At last, she saw a chance to ram one good shot down his throat. She soared up for the smash, but before she could connect, her legs became inextricably tangled with someone behind her.

"Oo-oof!" With a belly flop, she hit the unyielding ground. She lay dazed until her breath returned and she became aware of an overpowering mass pinning her down. "Mmmph," she moaned, and tried a tentative wiggle to dislodge the weight.

When she moved, a rusty-barbed-wire voice grated in her ear. "Feels like a horizontal move to me, North."

An hour later Bentley stood beneath a pulsing shower, washing away the dirt, yet unable to free herself from the feel of Reid pressed against her. Certain that he'd tripped her up on purpose, she knew she ought to be furious with him. But she couldn't summon up any genuine outrage.

Right after his blatant remark, he had turned very gentle and solicitous. He'd quickly rolled off and knelt beside her, helped her sit up, and finally, lifted her to stand. By that time a crowd had encircled them, but Reid continued to support her even after she insisted she'd only had the breath knocked out of her.

He led her to a chair and ordered someone to fetch ice water, which he used to bathe her forehead and neck. Bentley had felt ill at ease with all the attention and, showing more sensitivity than she'd expected from him, Reid had picked up on her discomfort. At that point, he inclined his head toward the buffet the caterers had finished setting out. As if he'd issued a command, their audience retreated.

Still shaky, she'd sat and watched him speak to several people, one of whom was Paul. Then he returned with two sacks and announced he would drive her home. Ignoring her protests, he hustled her into a pickup, swept aside an armful of styrofoam and paper, and nestled her amidst a mountain of fast-food debris.

Now he waited upstairs in her living room. Bentley shut off the water and toweled dry. She slipped on an orange-and-turquoise colored peasant dress and studied her bemused reflection, wishing she had stayed at the picnic. Grimy clothes and skinned elbows were a small price to pay to keep Reid out of her private domain. He had a way of filling up and taking charge of his surroundings.

"Come on," she scolded softly. "You can't hide in here all night." He'd be just the type to come after her, and she definitely didn't want him in her bedroom. She bent over and fluffed her damp curls, then climbed the stairs. Maybe she could convince him to return to the park.

After a detour through the living and dining rooms, she found him in the kitchen unwrapping food the caterers had sent. "Mr. Hunter, I appreciate your bringing me home, but don't you think you ought to go back and join the others?"

He looked at her as if she'd gone feeble-minded. "I hope you're hungry," he said, gesturing at the barbecue, fried chicken, assorted salads, chocolate cake, and watermelon wedges. "I thought we'd eat in here. It's cozier." He removed a colorful flower arrangement from her small breakfast table and placed it on the tea-cart. "What would you like to drink?"

Bentley wondered if he'd forgotten this was her home. "There's a bottle of wine in the refrigerator." She shook her head and her gaze followed him back to the kitchen where he found the glasses on the first try. He filled one with Chardonnay, the other with apple juice.

"You don't like wine?" she asked after taking a sip.

He dropped into one of the cane-backed chairs. "I don't drink much alcohol. I'm pretty hyper—restless and fidgety most of the time." He heaped food onto their plates. "Got a strange metabolism, I guess. Booze makes me even jumpier. Same with coffee and tea."

He picked up a fork, ending the disjointed recitation. Before he dug in, he caught her eye. "In fact, there's only one thing that calms me down at all." He smiled archly and sank his teeth into a link of smoked sausage.

Bentley stared at the food and told herself not to rise to his bait. As always, she couldn't stop herself. "Yes, warm milk works wonders, doesn't it?" She sampled a bite of ambrosia, grateful for its coolness.

Silent, he continued to watch her with an unfathomable expression in his amber-flecked eyes. If she intended to work for him, they were going to have to get a few things straight. "Why do you do it?"

He didn't pretend to misunderstand her question. "Damned if I know, North. There's something about you that drives me to say outrageous things. I don't plan to do it, even swear I won't, but they just slip out."

She rolled her eyes; he shrugged and gave her a contrite smile. "I absolve myself because I never get the best of you. The last word is usually yours, in case you haven't been keeping score." He pushed his plate aside.

"Still, it requires effort. I'd rather spend that energy on my work than trying to outtalk the boss." She paused so he'd know her next request was sincere. "So do you think we can declare a cease-fire?"

"We can call some sort of truce, I suppose, but there's an awful lot of inherent friction between us. It's inevitable that we'll rub up against each other."

The way he looked at her just then, she could almost feel them rubbing against each other, feel the ensuing sparks and consuming fire. Her body rippled with sensual awareness. To chase away the unwelcome sensation, she focused on a row of bright-pink potted geraniums on her balcony. The air around them crackled with electricity and magnetic force.

"See what I mean?" he asked, his voice gritty.

Oh, yes. It hit her with startling clarity. The wariness she'd felt when she first saw him hadn't been because he was a prospective employer, hadn't been because of what he'd said. It stemmed from something far more primitive—the instinctual parrying of male and female. The mating ritual. Bentley blinked. She shouldn't be thinking about such things in connection with this man.

"You feel it, too, don't you?"

She did, but wasn't about to admit it. This was a disaster waiting to happen. She'd wanted the job—needed it—more desperately than she had ever needed anything. Now her position was in jeopardy before she'd even begun.

Somehow she had to neutralize the dangerous, inexplicable attraction. She sat very still, hoping to appear calmer than she felt. "I think you must have your signals crossed, Mr. Hunter."

"Shame on you, North. I never figured you for a coward." He reached across the table and drew the tip of his index finger down the bridge of her nose, then to her mouth where it lingered.

A quivering excitement settled in her stomach. Her lips parted and she felt the warm rush of her breath against his finger. "Mr. Hunter . . ."

"It's Reid, Bentley." He stroked her jawline with the backs of his fingers, a motion as hypnotic as his low, spell-casting voice. "And you're going to say it a lot."

She closed her eyes and eased away from his inflaming touch. "Mr. Hunter," she tried again.

"Bentley, say my name."

She couldn't believe his voice deepened further, but it did. She shook her head, refusing to meet his eyes or respond to his demand.

"Say it!"

"Reid," she whispered.

"Yes," he said with a satisfied growl. "Delude yourself as long as you like, but that won't change the outcome. You're a smart lady. You know what's happening."

He stood and gathered the plates, leaving a dazed Bentley to stare after him. It didn't take a great intellect to figure out what was going on. She just didn't understand *why*. Even if he hadn't been her boss, he wasn't her type. He made her feel as though she had no control. Not of the situation, or her emotions, and especially not of him.

After he put the dishes in the dishwasher, he leaned

against the doorframe and smiled at her bewildered expression. "Come see me off. I have a plane to catch."

"A plane? To where?"

"Indianapolis."

"Oh, of course." She hated sounding so befuddled, like her brain was functioning at halfspeed. Maybe standing upright would get her back on track.

"It's my hometown."

"That's nice." No, upright didn't do the trick. She decided moving might work, so she led him down the stairs to her front door. She fretted that he'd try to kiss her and feared that she hadn't the strength to prevent it. When they reached the entry, she turned to face him.

"Oh, hell," he groaned, distress apparent in his voice.

"What's wrong?"

"Bentley, where's the closest bed?"

"Wha-a-t?" She'd half expected a pass, but figured he'd be a little more subtle than this.

"I'm not kidding, honey. I need a bed. Quick."

Bentley saw that he wasn't kidding. Perhaps he suffered from blackouts or seizures. Oh, Lord, what would she do if a giant like Reid passed out on her floor? She'd never be able to lift him. Her bedroom was on this level so she grabbed his hand and pulled him through the door.

"Don't worry," he assured her as he dropped like deadweight to the bed. "Two hours."

"Reid," she urged frantically, "wake up. Please." Her pummeling failed to rouse him. Bentley felt for the pulse in his neck. Strong and steady. She lifted one eyelid. Nothing abnormal there. But something wasn't right.

She grabbed her bedside phone and punched directory assistance. There was no answer at Marian Tolliver's number. She tried Jim Lawson next, blessing the modern wonders of call forwarding when Jim answered his cellular phone from the picnic.

When she explained what had happened, he chuckled. "He's only checked out for a couple of hours. No big deal."

"But what shall I do with him?"

He laughed again. "Bentley, Reid's sleep habits are as singular as everything else about him. He stays awake for hours, never goes to bed at a normal time. Then all at once the need to sleep hits him hard. He just crashes. I've seen him leave a board meeting and go to bed in his office. You've nothing to worry about."

After several more reassurances, she hung up. Once the adrenaline stopped flowing, Bentley sank into a nearby chair. Her legs felt like overcooked linguine and her hands would not stop shaking. She cast a glance at the man on her bed. How unfair that he was resting so peacefully after turning her into a basket case.

He sprawled half on his side, half on his stomach, with one of those troublesome long legs bent at the knee. His left arm stretched out, the hand dangling off the edge of the mattress. For such a tough-looking man, he had beautiful hands. Lean and tanned and strong, just like the rest of him.

Suddenly feeling like a voyeur, she jumped up, intent on leaving. She remained motionless, unable to take her eyes off him. Reid's face looked as if an impatient sculptor had tired of the project and abandoned it in the rough stage. It didn't matter that it wasn't a handsome face. Compared to his compelling presence, handsome seemed bland and uninteresting. Craggy. That's how a writer would describe the lines and seams. And he appealed to her far more than he should, Bentley admitted as she hurried out.

True to his word, two hours later Reid bounded up the stairs and found her lounging on the sofa, reading the latest novel in her favorite lady detective series. He looked bright-eyed and full of energy. "Sorry about that," he said, sounding less than apologetic. "Didn't have time to explain."

She sat up, dropping the book onto a cushion. "What you did was scare the life out of me. If I hadn't reached Jim, my next call was going to be 911."

"Jim told you I sometimes run out of steam without much warning?"

"Yes. Until then, I couldn't decide what to do with you."

His soft laugh sounded entirely too wicked. "But you see how fast I recharge?" He bent and pulled her up to face him. "I'm used to it." He looked at her, an undisguised glint in his eyes. "You might as well get used to it, too, Bentley."

His voice evoked urges that weren't at all civilized, and she fought to subdue the thrill his words kindled. "I'm sure it won't affect me at all, Mr. Hunter."

"I guess you're right. It never happens while I'm making love."

_____ THREE _____

Bentley was already awake when her radio clicked on at six. She'd been thinking about the day ahead, anxious to start working again. She had left New York over a month ago, long enough for the nightmares to have begun subsiding. Each day she dreaded a ringing phone a little bit less. The challenge of her new job would help dispel the lingering effects of her ordeal. But her new boss might prove to be a bigger challenge than she'd ever faced.

At five minutes before eight, Bentley gave her name to the receptionist. On her two interviews, she hadn't been taken on a tour so she had no idea which building housed the legal department.

"Yes, Ms. North, Mr. Hunter is expecting you in his office. You know the way, don't you?"

She thanked the efficient young woman and took the back way out of the main building. Striding down the narrow walkway, she wondered if Reid gave all his beginning employees an official welcome. His methods were radically different from those of most executives in his position. She hoped he would confine this meeting to a discussion of her duties and not remind her of the last time she'd seen him.

He had a knack for saying things that completely unnerved her. The other night when he'd informed her he never fell asleep while making love, Bentley had colored like a naive schoolgirl. She resented him for reducing her to that. Resented, too, her body's heated reaction to the visual fantasy of him in her bed, making good on the promise she'd seen in his eyes.

"He's in the shower," Marian Tolliver informed Bentley when she reached Reid's office. "He'll be out shortly." At Bentley's questioning look, she explained. "He just got in from Indianapolis and came straight from the airport."

Bentley nodded. "He mentioned he was going there—" A sharp buzz interrupted her.

"He's ready for you," Mrs. T. said, motioning to the door of the inner office.

Bentley felt the strange little tremor she had come to associate with facing Reid, but she entered assertively, determined to disregard her sudden case of nerves. She stopped just inside the door, her hand still wrapped around the knob.

He stood before a mirror knotting a striped silk tie. She felt sure she must have witnessed that masculine ritual before, but watching Reid do it stirred something deep inside her, something that had no right to intrude when she needed to concentrate on her job. "Good morning," she said, glad her vocal cords and stomach weren't connected.

"Ms. North." He pointed to a chair that faced his desk, then finished the tie and draped his jacket over a chair back.

She didn't like to sit when he was still standing. It gave him too much of an advantage. This time, however, she planned to be as acquiescent as possible and hope to avoid a repeat of their previous confrontations. She sat with her spine very straight, sending a message in body language.

Reid paced back and forth behind the desk, both hands jammed in his pockets. "Okay," he said without looking at her. "For the first few weeks you'll work directly for me. That means I'll tell you what to do, and when you're finished, you'll report back to me." He stopped and faced her, as if expecting a protest. "Any problem with that?"

"None at all, Mr. Hunter."

"If I'm satisfied at the end of that time, you'll go on to legal and Jim Lawson will take over. It'll be up to him to decide where he wants to assign you permanently. In the meantime, you can work in the law library."

"I'm sure I can manage just fine." On the surface, the exchange was quite agreeable. Bentley could almost believe she'd imagined their prior difficulties.

"Good." He handed her several typewritten pages. "Start with this."

She took a cursory glance at the first page and blanched. So her trial wasn't an idle threat, either. Too bad he hadn't selected something more constructive than verifying antitrust case cites. This was busy work, even for a novice clerk. She couldn't forego a small jibe, because his project narrowly missed being insulting. She wanted him to know he hadn't fooled her. "I'll whip through these in an embarrassingly short time, Mr. Hunter."

He dropped into his chair and smiled at her as if they

shared an amusing secret. "I'm glad to hear that,
North. I like optimistic people. When you're ready to
report to me, call Mrs. T. and make an appointment.
Until then, she'll show you where you'll be working."
He nodded toward the door in unspoken dismissal.

It was a gesture he rarely needed to make, Bentley
guessed. Wise employees probably learned how to read
his signals and she was no exception. She followed as
Marian led her to yet another building and gave her
two keys, one for the front door, one to the library.
With a smile, Mrs. Tolliver eyed the work Bentley
tossed on the table. "Would you like a bit of free
advice?"

Curious, Bentley nodded her assent.

"Don't be discouraged by the first couple of things
he gives you to do." She patted the stack of papers
and said, "Just remember, he'll place less importance
on what you do than on how you do it."

Bentley's shoulders sagged. More games. "I'm afraid
I'll have to work harder than most to impress Mr.
Hunter." She realized the stark truth of her statement.
Reid would never let her forget she was on probation
as an employee.

Marian's grin was infectious. "Oh, he's already impressed, but that won't give you any advantage here."
She pointed to the shelves of law books surrounding
them. "Whatever else is between you two, you'll have
to do the job to keep it."

Seeing Bentley about to protest, Mrs. T. held up her
hand and shook her head. "I didn't mean to imply that
you're not competent. I know you are or he'd never
have hired you." The smile flashed again. "I just recognize that there's something more."

"Oh, no. How did you—"

"Dear, I've been widowed since '85. Before that I had twenty-seven delightful years with a man who was much like Reid. That's why I know how to handle him. Their type doesn't ensure a very peaceful existence, but who wants that anyway? Give me excitement—passion—any day." When Bentley didn't reply, Marian nodded and left her alone.

By midafternoon Bentley suspected she'd once again allowed Reid to prod her into speaking too hastily. She worked until nine that night and was convinced of it. "Face facts," she lectured herself, "you shot off your mouth and now you can't deliver." She had to learn one thing in a hurry—there was no future in second-guessing Reid Hunter. The next lesson was to learn to keep her mouth shut when he was anywhere near.

After her third day, Bentley had only progressed to the second phase of her project. At this rate she might be stuck on one problem for the entire trial period. Devious was the kindest word she could use to describe her boss. What had seemed like child's play had turned into a complex maze of legal precedents, each one leading her up against a whole new set of obstacles.

She looked at the clock. After eleven, and she hadn't eaten dinner. Food would have to wait until tomorrow, she decided, yawning as she massaged her tense shoulder muscles. The way she felt, she'd be lucky to make it home. Maybe a short nap would revive her. Perhaps she could even work a little longer. If she rested . . .

Reid checked his watch when he locked his office building for the night. Eleven-twenty. Time enough to get some sleep if he needed it, with plenty of time to make it to Dallas for the breakfast meeting. At that hour, there wouldn't be much traffic and he could turn his Porsche loose to eat up the miles between cities. He could just as easily fly, but he loved the thrill of speeding through the night in a finely tuned automobile.

Aside from work, it was one of the few pleasures he granted himself.

When he reached the parking lot, he spotted an unfamiliar white sports car. Alert to the possibility of a break-in, he scanned the area. Then he noticed a single lighted window in one of the buildings.

"Law library," he muttered, striding swiftly in that direction. "It better not be who I think it is." But he knew before he entered that he'd find Bentley. What he didn't comprehend was his violent surge of anger.

"What the hell do you think you're doing?" he demanded in a thunderous voice as he flung the door open. He saw her and the anger died, replaced by an emotion that was as foreign as it was powerful. She looked so vulnerable that he felt a fierce need to take care of her, protect her, comfort her. An idiotic urge, he warned himself. He'd never known any woman who needed those things less than Bentley Brighton North.

She raised her head, blinking as she tried to focus on what had awakened her. He reached to lift her gently and smiled when she snuggled up to his warmth. Reid took several deep breaths. He eased himself down on a couch, cradling her against him, careful not to disturb her.

God, she was beautiful like this, so feminine and tempting. It was all he could do to rein in his desire to touch her all over. His fingers flexed with the need to learn every soft curve, each sweet indentation beneath the clingy peach silk. He settled for just holding her . . . while she slept.

He wanted Bentley, all of her. He admired her

shrewd intellect, her sense of humor, the self-confidence she radiated. He even enjoyed feeling the sting of her sometimes waspish tongue. But tonight he could think of better uses for it. And he wanted her to look at him with something other than anger.

"Bentley? Honey, can you wake up?"

"Mmm, no-o-o."

Bentley heard a deep chuckle rumble in her ear. A voice urged, "Come on." Something nibbled at the same ear. "Open your eyes, sweetheart."

"Go a-way," she mumbled, ineffectually swatting at the pesky nibbler. The laugh echoed again and she finally began to edge toward wakefulness. "What?" She sat up suddenly and blinked in sleepy disorientation. How on earth had she gotten onto the leather sofa? And why was she sitting on her employer's lap? "Oh! Mr. Hunter!"

"Reid," he corrected as he brushed the hair away from her face and tucked it behind her ear. "Don't you remember falling asleep at the table?"

"Mmm, yes, I guess." Her voice was still fuzzy, but her body was aware, and warm from the close contact with him. Too warm. She needed to stop this now, but she was so tired, and his arms held her so insistently. "I think it's time for me to go home." She struggled against the confining bonds.

"Uh uh. Not yet." His tongue slid along the perimeter of her ear, dipped inside, then traced the outline again.

"Aaah," Bentley sighed, and melted against his solidity, even as she cautioned herself to stop him immediately. How wonderful it would be to float endlessly on this cloud of sensual bliss. But she couldn't.

"Don't," she protested in a voice that she meant to sound more reproving.

"Don't what? Touch you? Kiss you? But I have to, Bentley. I can't wait any longer." His hand slipped around her waist and turned her toward him as his lips descended slowly to claim her mouth.

The merest hint of lips touching overwhelmed her. She felt possessed. But, oh, such sweet possession, she thought as her lips softened and she answered his demand.

His mustache teased her sensitive skin while his mouth moved with delicious intent over hers, moistening, probing, penetrating. When his hands plunged into her hair and brought her closer, Bentley murmured her acceptance. She felt her will slip away, stolen by his languid, stroking tongue.

She was hardly aware that she embraced him, lacing her fingers together behind his neck. She knew only that she must hold fast to the source of this magic— magic that heightened with every demanding thrust of his tongue.

She felt herself drifting, being absorbed by Reid's potent call to her senses. No kiss, no man, had ever stormed her defenses this quickly and completely. Warning signals jangled, bringing her fully awake.

There were so many reasons she shouldn't let him kiss her this way. The man was too arrogant, too confident. Even more distressing, he was her boss. Most of all, he was making her enjoy it too much. Where had her common sense and good judgment gone? "No!" She broke the embrace and scrambled to 'her feet.

"What the hell?" Reid stood and grasped her arm, turning her to face him. "Why the great escape?"

"That should be obvious," she told him in a voice cool enough to establish the proper distance between them.

"I must be dense. You'll have to explain the obvious."

She eyed him skeptically, but he did look puzzled. "Mr. Hunter, I'm your employee. And this—" She motioned to the sofa. "There's a term for this sort of thing. One I don't care to have associated with my name." She smoothed her disheveled clothing with her free hand. "It was only a kiss and if it never happens again, there won't be a problem."

"It'll happen again."

"It won't!"

"I'll show you." His arms went around her and he pulled her tight against the taut length of him.

Bentley shivered when her breasts touched his hard chest. She had to get away, but it took all her strength to free herself. She glared at him and ordered in an icy tone, "Stop manhandling me!"

He advanced, forcing her to step back until her legs bumped against the table. "But I will handle you. Every sweet inch of you. And what's more, you'll want me to." His thumb and index finger tipped her chin up so she couldn't avoid his heated gaze. "You'll ask me . . . maybe even beg."

"I've never begged for anything. I doubt I'd be very good at it."

He grinned at her hauteur. "I imagine you'll do it like you do everything else. Going after what you want with your eyes wide open. And *I*, Ms. North, am the one man who can give it to you."

"On a cold day, Mr. Hunter. On a cold day."

Reid stared at the door for a few seconds after it

crashed into the wall from the force of Bentley's exit. Then his grin spread into a full, knowing smile. "I don't think so, honey. I think it'll be the hottest damn day of both our lives."

By seven the next morning Bentley was in the law library, her thoughts involuntarily drawn back to the previous evening. How suddenly her whole existence had turned into a series of confrontations with Reid. After each one she swore she'd never again let him provoke her, yet somehow he always did. She had to put a stop to it.

She supposed some might label his treatment of her as sexual harassment. It never crossed Bentley's mind to accuse him of that. She hadn't been at Maverick long, but the Hunter reputation was legend. He was universally praised for treating *all* his employees with respect and fairness. There was no indication that he'd ever behaved less than professionally with any woman who worked for him.

Why had he singled her out? She couldn't allow herself to believe that he was seriously interested in her. Even if she were willing—and she absolutely was not—an involvement would only complicate an already muddled situation.

She jumped up from the couch, the scene of last night's devastating kiss. She had never been in such a compromising position before, which was why she'd fled. But she hadn't escaped. Reid had caught up with her in the parking lot and lectured her all the way to her car about the danger of being alone in an unlocked building so late.

Unnerved, Bentley had driven away before he had finished scolding her. So she'd been totally surprised when he followed her home and waited until the garage door closed behind her. Coming from any other man, the gesture would have struck her as sweet.

As he'd been when he woke her with gentle touches and whispered endearments, his words low and husky like a lover's. His kiss had been that of a lover, too, deep and intimate and exciting.

She struck the table with her fist. This wasn't the place for such fantasies, nor was he the man. Bentley had reached the point where she was ready to settle down. But she'd want to be certain that the man she fell in love with was willing to devote as much time to their relationship as she would.

Reid Hunter would not be capable of that degree of commitment. Business was his only obsession, his true mistress. Professional ethics aside, that alone was reason enough to avoid an emotional entanglement. She had to concentrate on doing the job and be sure to keep that the only contact with her boss.

Fueled by new resolve, she finished the project by mid-afternoon. When she called Mrs. Tolliver, she learned Reid was out of town until Friday morning. Marian put her down for an appointment late the next day and relayed Reid's next set of instructions.

Bentley hung up the phone very carefully. She wanted to hurl it against the wall. "Stupid waste of time," she said through gritted teeth. "Looking for pending antitrust legislation in the Congressional Record."

She was still incensed when she went to his office the next afternoon. He was wearing a path in the Kirman rug, shouting into a cordless phone. Bentley put her purse and the report on a table and chose a corner chair away from the line of fire.

He had on faded jeans, a plaid shirt with the sleeves rolled up, and scuffed Dingo boots. Wherever he'd been, he hadn't shaved and he had spent the time outdoors. His face and arms were bronzed, and several days' growth of beard now framed the heavy mustache, making him appear even more like an outlaw. He ought to look out of place amid the burnished wood, oil paintings, and antique rugs, but he didn't.

And she knew why. Reid epitomized power, a commodity that transcended clothes or furnishings and made them mere substitutes for the real thing. Bentley recognized this; she'd met many powerful people before. But she had never felt the effect quite so keenly as she did with Reid.

All at once she could feel him staring back at her. "Well, did you find your second job as easy as the first?"

"Routine," she said, bent on staying calm.

"That's good. Give me a ride home in those fancy wheels and we'll discuss your next assignment. I'll even spring for dinner on the way."

Big bad wolf. She wasn't gullible enough to fall for that old routine.

"Business, Bentley," he said, cutting off the excuse she'd been fabricating. "Have you forgotten who's boss?"

Her mouth tightened. "Of course not. Sir." She retrieved her purse and plopped the stack of papers she'd brought squarely in the center of his desk. "Shall we go?"

On the way to the car, she pondered the consequences of refusing to have dinner with him, then decided it wasn't worth the effort. When the time came to defy Reid, she'd have to pick the issue carefully and wear her fastest guns.

He folded his long frame into the Jag's low seat. "Cut down to West Gray and we'll stop by the Black-Eyed Pea. I'm not dressed for anywhere fancy." He saw her eye his clothes. "I've been out in the Gulf, touring offshore oil rigs for a couple of days."

"I see." In her job interview he had thrown out the hypothetical question about acquiring an oil company. Perhaps he meant to do just that. It would fit his pattern of diversifying at random, always venturing into new, unrelated fields.

"Most people would warn you that's the absolutely worst kind of investment these days."

"I never listen to 'most people.' Wouldn't have gotten anywhere paying attention to all the things *they* said I couldn't do."

Challenge. He thrived on it. Was she just one more?

During the next hour he conveniently forgot why he had insisted on the meeting. Instead, they discussed basketball. Reid had bought the perennially cellar-dwelling Houston Titans franchise at the end of last season. He talked enthusiastically about his plans for the team's resurrection. Since Bentley was a dedicated fan it was easy for her to get caught up in his excitement.

When they finished eating he gave her directions to his house, which turned out to be a short distance from the offices. Located in the Heights, one of Houston's older neighborhoods, it was surrounded by beautifully restored homes, some with plaques proclaiming their historical significance. Reid's was not one of those. His, he informed her with classic understatement, needed a little fixing up.

"Oh, this poor thing." Bentley could imagine the neighbors cringing each time they looked at it. A three-sided porch sagged and the exterior hadn't seen a paintbrush in several decades. It stood out like a frumpy dowager among a gathering of lace-clad debutantes.

"Why don't you come in? Maybe you can give me some pointers."

His invitation sounded harmless. She forgot this was the enemy camp. He unlocked the oak front door and showed her inside. "Where are the walls?"

He laughed at her horrified look. "Piled up in the dining room." He pointed to a stack of sheetrock blocking the double doorway.

"A redo. Quite a few of my friends are knee-deep in renovations, too. Here and in West U."

Reid plucked a cap off a nail and fitted it over his thick hair. Bentley jerked her eyes away as soon as she read the cap's printed message, *It Takes Studs to Build Houses*. He grinned and she knew he'd seen the heat rush to her face and neck.

"Seven years ago when I bought this, a buddy of mine got us these work caps and volunteered to help. He finally quit coming last year. Said he'd given up on my beginning, much less completing the project."

How could anyone tolerate such chaos that long? "You've lived like this for seven years?"

"Afraid so. I can't find time to get it done." He walked toward the dining room, kicking up little puffs of dust with his heels.

"Couldn't you hire someone to do the work for you?"

"I could, but that would defeat the purpose." He turned to face her again. "I'm a tinkerer. Guess it's the engineer in me. I like to take things apart and put them back together so they're better than before." He rapped his knuckles on an exposed two-by-four. "When I'm through, this place will not only be structurally but *visually* superior to the original."

"And until then, you don't mind living like this?"

He hesitated for a moment, his perplexed expression leading her to believe that he'd never questioned the lack of comfort. "If I spent much time here, I guess it might bother me, but I'm out of town at least half the time. When I'm not, I spend most nights at the office. I have everything I need there. Not much reason to come home."

Depression settled on Bentley like a tangible weight. He'd only confirmed what she already knew. He had no life apart from business. She wished that fact didn't bother her so much. "No one works all the time. What about weekends?"

"They're like every other day to me. I'm either at the office or not in Houston."

Worse than she'd suspected. "You never jump in the car and go to the beach? Or over to the hill country just for the pure pleasure of it?"

He shoved his hands into the back pockets of his jeans, stretching the snug denim even tauter across his hips. Bentley forced her gaze downward, dismayed that his unconscious act caused such a riot in her midsection. They both watched him scoot a nail back and forth with the toe of his boot.

At last he spoke without meeting her eyes. "Last year a friend convinced me to buy a house on the water in Rockport. It's directly across from his, and he promised it was a deal I couldn't pass up." He ducked his head even lower. "For all I know, it may be in sorrier shape than this place."

"You own a house you've never seen?"

"Mmm, but I'm going to try to get down there soon. Maybe in the fall."

"What *do* you do for fun?" she asked, knowing his answer would further depress her.

"Work is my fun. I enjoy what I do so much that it doesn't seem like work at all." An almost childlike wonder filled his eyes. "Not once in the eight years since I started my company have I wanted to be doing anything else."

Bentley wished she had refused to come here. But in her wildest imagination she could never have predicted she would see his chosen lifestyle as a personal rejection.

What in heaven's name was wrong with her? Why did she care how he lived? The answers came quickly and she sucked in a breath to combat the sharp pang of regret. Whether she wanted to admit it or not, and unwelcome as it was, she had begun to nurture the hope that, because of her, Reid might want to change.

It was ridiculous, of course, the kind of illusion that had been breaking women's hearts for eons. Such dangerous hopes were destined to bring disappointment and pain.

Reid had made his choices; he was content with them. And because he was, he could never be the kind of man with whom she could build a future.

FOUR

The silence lengthened while Bentley tried to assure herself that Reid's revelation was for the best. Weaving romantic dreams around her boss made no sense. Careers and reputations had been ruined by that sort of folly.

Reid must have picked up on her pensive mood. He touched her elbow and said, "Let's get on with the tour."

Though she tried not to, Bentley decorated every room in her mind. The house had so much charm it would provide a cozy haven if only someone would pay it the proper attention. Her own townhouse was lovely, but this was a real home, the kind of place to spend a lifetime.

Upstairs she found the first sign of progress. The two front bedrooms had been joined to form a master suite, and she saw at once that Reid did understand the house's potential. Indigo-blue walls contrasted with ivory woodwork and bleached oak floors. The colors, along with accents of antique red, were also used in the connecting bath, dressing room, and study. The end result was dramatic and striking.

An unpalatable thought chilled her. Suppose he had remodeled only this area to impress his female companions. While she could not imagine Reid cooking dinner for a woman, she could all too clearly picture him bedding one.

To banish that disturbing idea, Bentley squinted at the wall of bookcases. Her leather-bound Trollope novels would be the perfect balance for his heavy engineering texts. On the opposite end, her porcelain flowers could add a color contrast to his scrimshaw collection. Despite her mental arranging, the image of Reid with another woman remained stubbornly entrenched in her mind's eye.

The bed, with its red-and-blue plaid comforter, looked so big and masculine and . . . inviting.

"I completed this months ago. You're the first person who's seen it."

He stood directly behind her, his voice low and hypnotic in her ear. Heart pounding, she turned to look at him, determined to conceal her smile of relief. "Should I be flattered?" she asked, using flippancy as a defense against the powerful emotions he stirred.

"Maybe you should be, but you're not. What *would* impress you, Bentley? Is there anything I could do to earn a compliment?"

"I'd guess your ego is healthy enough to thrive without any encouragement from me." The shift in conversation made her uneasy and she hurried into the hall, intent on getting back downstairs.

His hand clasped her arm, gentle yet restraining. "You're probably right, but haven't you ever wanted something you didn't need?"

Unfortunately, yes! Right this minute. Bentley's perception of him increased, her senses alert to every move, each nuance. She tried to discourage herself from wanting Reid's lips on hers. Still, she craved them, and with an urgency that she'd never experienced in all her twenty-eight years. But that was the last thing she needed.

"Part of growing up is learning you don't get everything you want."

"Then I'm glad I haven't grown up completely. I like to think I can have whatever I want."

"And have you never been disappointed?" Her breathless voice betrayed too much.

"I've found that if I want something badly enough, I can figure out a way to get it."

There it was again, the confidence that bordered on arrogance. But as Bill would say, "It ain't bragging if you can do it." Time after time, Reid had shown the world he could do most anything. Which only made her feel more vulnerable.

"Why don't you show me the yard? I'm much better at landscaping than decorating." Anything to put some distance between her and his stirring touch.

They passed through the antiquated kitchen and a small back porch into a large overgrown yard. Bentley loved flowers and blooming shrubs. She salivated at the prospect of what she could accomplish with this derelict plot.

Immediately lost in visions of gardenias and crape myrtles, azaleas and roses, camellias and jasmine, she closed her eyes and inhaled the potpourri of imagined fragrances.

"You're picturing it in bloom, aren't you?"

Bentley jumped slightly when his voice intruded.

She'd almost forgotten she wasn't alone. "Why, yes. How. could you tell?"

"Don't forget, I've seen your home. It's obvious you like flowers. The place is full of them."

"I can't explain why, but when I'm surrounded by flowers they make me happy. I've always loved gardening."

He drew her to an old-fashioned park bench and seated her with unexpected courtliness. "Maybe when I get to this part, you can give me some advice. I don't know the first thing about landscaping." He sat at the opposite end, leaving an unthreatening amount of space between them.

Instinct told Bentley she ought to discourage this kind of familiarity, but unlikely as it seemed, she felt at ease with Reid for the first time since she'd met him. It was probably a dangerous delusion, but one she wanted to prolong. "I'll be glad to help you when you're ready."

He smiled at her and his hand rested lightly on her shoulder. "Good. I'll hold you to that." The hand moved to her neck where he idly kneaded her nape. "I hope you'll be as receptive to my next request."

Bentley stiffened. She should never have permitted herself to relax. "What request?"

"Will you have dinner with me tomorrow night?" As if anticipating her reluctance, he added, "I promise to be on my best behavior."

She let a silent stream of air whisper over her parted lips, relieved that she had a legitimate excuse. "I can't."

"Does that translate *won't*?" His voice remained soft, but it carried an unmistakable demand.

Bentley risked a smile only because encroaching darkness protected her from his penetrating eyes. "One of my closest friends is getting married tomorrow evening. I'll be at the wedding and reception.''

"A wedding. Seems like most people I know have quit doing that sort of thing.''

Did she detect a trace of cynicism lurking beneath the level tone? "Haven't you heard? Marriage is back in vogue. Weddings and honeymoons and babies are all the rage again.'' She'd sure been surrounded by her share lately.

"And you, Miss North?'' he asked in a husky voice, guaranteed to entice. "Is that what you're looking for?''

Like the absolute quiet that precedes a thunderstorm, the atmosphere between them sizzled with expectency. Of all the topics she might discuss with Reid, matrimony was at the bottom of the list. "My stepfather says something every couple should save for old age is marriage.''

He laughed, but wasn't diverted. "You plan to take his advice?''

"No, not really. It's just that I haven't, uh, there hasn't been—''

"Any reason to get married?''

"Yes,'' she whispered. "That's it.''

"And when you meet the man who makes you feel differently, someone who makes you want things you've never wanted before, then you'll settle down?''

"Yes,'' she said again. Had he just given his own reasons for staying single? "I suppose you're often asked why there is no Mrs. Hunter.''

He gave a disparaging grunt. "You can't imagine how often. Beats me why complete strangers are interested in whether I have a wife or not. What gives them the right to ask in the first place? They're worse than busybodies, they're vultures.''

Didn't he understand that people were naturally curious about someone who'd started a company at twenty-six and eight years later had built it into a conglomerate with worldwide recognition? He was an American success story—part pioneer, part outlaw, with a dash of folk hero.

She recalled the research she'd done on him to prepare for her first interview. His business deals were documented in detail. She hadn't, however, found any photos or gossipy articles that painted him as a playboy. On the contrary, there was a noticeable lack of information about his private life. But there had been a few other references, and she couldn't resist taunting him with them.

"What do you expect when you keep turning up on Most Eligible Bachelor lists?"

That inspired an especially pungent oath, followed by a quick, "Sorry," in the next breath. "I tend to get violent on this subject."

Bentley smiled. She found Reid's verbal slip and subsequent apology oddly endearing because it was the kind of thing she'd often heard Bill do. "You don't think it's an honor to be a Most Eligible?"

"What I *think* is it's a bunch of crap. The whole idea is so stupid, it doesn't deserve mentioning." He started to say more, then clapped his mouth shut. "How did we get on this subject anyway?"

Reid wasn't easily manipulated, but she'd been able to switch the focus to him. Her success was short-lived.

"Think you're clever, don't you? But now . . ." He stood and pulled her up at the same time. "You owe me one for letting myself be distracted."

"Only one?" She'd meant it to sound playful. It didn't come out that way. Like much of what she said to him, it seemed laced with challenge.

"Mmm," he murmured, drawing her closer with an almost weightless touch of his hand on her arm. "One of these." He bent to nuzzle aside the silk blouse, laying a moist track of kisses along her collarbone until his tongue found the hollow and lingered. "And one of these." His mouth lightly brushed hers, hovered there to tantalize before his tongue slipped past her parted lips and began to stroke.

Bentley swayed. She urged herself to fight the intrusion and the avid yearning it created. But she was powerless to stop it. Indeed, she wanted more. She grasped his arms to steady herself; her hands stayed to explore firm biceps, then continued their trail of discovery to his chest. He was hard, uncompromisingly male, yet she felt the slight tremors her touch caused, felt his heart's cadence drum against her hand.

"And one . . ." His words were lost in her mouth as his hand slowly, but without hesitation, covered her breast.

All sensation rushed to converge at that heated point of contact. The thin material of her blouse was no protection against his searing touch. He cupped and lifted the soft fullness to graze his chest, and when his thumb glided in lazy arcs over the tip, Bentley moaned.

Reid took the sound into his mouth and gave it back to her as his thumb continued its gently mesmerizing assault. He shifted then, pulling her tighter against him, his body branding hers with the unmistakable evidence of his desire.

Shaken by what she'd allowed to happen, she jumped back. "Reid, please. Don't do this to me."

"I'm not *doing* anything to you." His hips thrust once and he held her still to absorb it. "This just *is*. And neither of us can do a thing to stop it. Hell, I can't even control it."

Eyes pleading, she shook her head in silent rejection. He'd have none of it. "We both felt it that first day and it's only gotten stronger." His fingers trailed across her lips. "You may not be able to accept that yet, but you damned sure can't deny it."

Bentley trembled, precariously close to tears. She clenched her eyes shut, reminding herself that she couldn't cry, especially not in front of Reid. Somehow he'd turn tears into a weapon against her and she was defenseless enough already.

"No, I can't deny it," she said, her tone wooden. "How can I?" She stepped back and brought his hands to her breasts, where her nipples brazenly defied two layers of silk. She heard his sharp intake of breath.

His hands shook, his voice wavered. "What are you saying?"

"That I want you. So much it scares me. And since this need is not something I can . . . manage, it scares me even more." It was the unvarnished truth, and she was going to pay dearly for telling him.

"Do I hear a 'but' coming?" His voice was still shaky, though tempered with wariness.

"Reid, if you care anything for me, if you respect me at all, don't force this. I want my job, want to work at Maverick. But if you persist, you'll not leave me any choice. I'll resign."

"This," he said, fitting them together again, "doesn't have anything to do with your job."

Typical male reaction. "How can you say that? Of course it does!" She took a deep breath and expelled a lengthy sigh. Why couldn't he see her point? "I'm a professional, my career is very important to me. Even if you don't believe it, I've worked hard to get where I am."

"I have no problem with that, Bentley. I realize I may come off sounding like a chauvinist, but I'm not. I have always tried to judge every employee on his or her ability and performance. Nothing else. I think I've been reasonably successful at it."

"If that's true, you must understand that I cannot have an affair with my boss. It would go against everything I believe in."

"And you must understand that I want you. Call me every name you can think of, but make no mistake. I will have you." How effortlessly he lapsed into the role of powerful executive. "If you can't find a way to reconcile that with working for me, then resign. Get yourself another job and our dilemma will be solved."

"You arrogant, self-centered bas—"

"I'm a man, Bentley, before everything else. And I want you as much as I've ever wanted anything. That ought to tell you how this will turn out."

"Oh! You . . ." she fumed, too infuriated to come up with a contemptible enough description.

His eyes closed and he sighed. "When I first interviewed you, I had a feeling this would come up sooner or later, but I hired you anyway. You're a Maverick kind of person, my kind of employee." His drawl became more evident. "Now, if you issue an ultimatum, make me choose between the lawyer and the woman . . ."

Darkness didn't diminish the predatory fire in his eyes, and she knew what he was thinking. "I see how you got where you are. Just grab hold of the throat and keep squeezing until your opponent gives up."

He placed a light kiss on her temple. "I don't want to pressure you. I honestly don't. I want you to work for me, and I want us to be lovers. For you, I can break the rules and do both simultaneously." He held up his hands. "How about if I promise not to chase you around any desks or lure you into the bed in my office?"

Bentley resented his making sport of her predicament. He was determined to have his way regardless of the consequences to her, as if she were some spineless, mindless bimbo. "You just don't get it, do you?"

"I get it. And I'm willing to compromise . . . to a degree. But I won't give you up. Not for my company, not for your career, not for anything."

She wanted to tell him she wasn't his to give up, but antagonizing him further would only prolong her ordeal. Reid thrived on adversity and she had no intention of waving herself like a red flag. "You want too much."

"I won't settle for less."

"Then I guess we're at an impasse because I can't go along with what you want."

"At some point, you won't be able to stop it." In the diffused glow of a streetlight, she saw him run both hands through his thick hair, then his fingers massaged his neck. "I know now isn't the time, but this is going to happen, Bentley. We'll be together because neither of us is a masochist." He kissed her again, sweetly but thoroughly, and looped his arm around her waist.

Sides touching, they walked down the driveway toward her car. "Are you sure I can't see you tomorrow night?"

"I . . . yes. I do have the wedding." She battled the wild urge to stay with him now, even after what had just happened. Or heaven help her, because of it.

"All right. But I'll go crazy thinking about you dancing with some pretty boy in a monkey suit." His voice dropped to a raspy whisper. "I'm damn close to carrying you up the stairs and ending this torture."

Bentley knew his pulling a Rhett Butler was not the solution, but she found herself wishing he'd follow through. She'd never been swept away, and right now, she wanted to be. It was madness.

When he opened her car door, she sank into the seat and grabbed the wheel. She desperately needed to latch on to something solid, cling to something real other than Reid.

He leaned over and his mustache feathered her cheek. "Forget all the reasons against it, honey. This is one fight I can't let you win."

Bentley reached for her seat belt, twisted the key, and shifted into reverse. His shadow was so long, so dominant, she stared out the windshield, refusing to look at him. "If I let you win, I'm afraid there'll be nothing left of me."

Driving home, Bentley tried to formulate her next move. She could resign and forfeit an interesting job with an exciting company, the sort of position she needed right now. Despite the humdrum tasks she'd been assigned so far, she knew that wouldn't last long. Once Reid had finished his "initiation," the work promised to be stimulating. But staying automatically put her at great risk.

She had kept telling herself she could handle Reid, an assumption she now saw as naive. He was about as controllable as a natural disaster and infinitely more dangerous. If only she didn't feel the overwhelming attraction to him, she might be able to resist. Tonight had shown her how defenseless she was against his appeal.

Basically, she was in a situation where she had no good alternatives, only choices she did not want to face. Perhaps if she delayed a decision long enough, the problem would resolve itself. Procrastination was foreign to Bentley, but she was in a bind.

Reid had said he spent half his time out of town. If she could elude him the other half, she just might be able to hang on to her job as well as restore some tranquility to her personal life.

Displaying incredibly bad timing, the singer on her cassette tape bemoaned being "good and lost in a fool's paradise."

Saturday night as Bentley dressed for Robin's wedding, she looked to the evening ahead. Her pale-rose silk dress shimmered to midcalf, and she liked the way it contrived to look both demure and provocative. She stepped in front of a cheval mirror and smoothed the ivory lace that banded the hip. How would Reid react if he saw her now?

"Forget him," she ordered herself sternly. "At least you don't have to worry about running into him tonight."

For a few blessed hours, she didn't think of Reid once. The ceremony at a large downtown cathedral and the reception that followed at the home of Robin's father was almost like a reunion. Bentley saw people she'd lost contact with years before, when they'd all gone in different directions.

By midnight most of the crowd had departed and she walked down the block to her car, feeling tired yet too keyed up to sleep. When she was in this state, there was only one sure fire means to wind down. She headed for an all-night florist.

At a red light on Westheimer, a large, mean-looking black motorcycle pulled up beside her, so close it crowded into her lane rather than the inner one where it belonged. "That figures," she muttered. In this part of town cruising in all its varied forms was a favorite pastime on late Saturday nights.

Gloved hands revved the powerful engine until its vibrations rocked her car, insisting that she recognize the rider's presence. After the light turned green she glanced over and nodded to give him the go-ahead.

Her eyes collided with an inky void. He wore a black helmet and his face was hidden behind a smoked visor. Against her will, Bentley was lured by the aura of mystery, ominous and at the same time intriguing.

Behind her, an impatient driver honked, jarring her back to reality. She raced forward and so did the cycle. She slowed and the Harley did, too, matching her pace. She pushed the pedal to the floor and when he did likewise, she braked and cut sharply into the left lane. Without signaling, she swerved onto Buffalo Speedway, then proceeded to the florist's, certain she'd sent the mysterious rider off to harass someone else.

It had been a brief interlude that unfortunately left her more wired than ever.

Inside, Bentley browsed leisurely before filling her arms with anthuriums, stargazer lilies, and liatris. Concentrating on the floral arrangements she intended to make banished all thoughts of the phantom cyclist. At the first traffic light, he rolled up beside her again.

A tremor rippled over her, but she wasn't sure if it was fear or another kind of adrenaline-producing response. This time she studied him, noting details she'd missed before. Even though the early-morning air was warm and heavy, he wore a jacket. Instead of the regulation biker style, his was a leather windbreaker that she could tell would be sensuously soft if she touched it.

Her eyes shifted down, down past muscled thighs encased in well-worn denim to . . . Just below the knee, her gaze locked on supple riding boots, their flat heels assertively planted on the pavement to support the straining machine he sat astride. "Uh-*huh*!" she whispered, moistening her lower lip. If anything could reduce her to a puddle, it was a long-legged man in black leather riding boots.

Where had her common sense gone? Excited by, drooling over—almost flirting with—a dark stranger who might well pull out a gun and blow her away. But she sat transfixed, as if mesmerized.

She retraced an upward route, along terrain that began to look familiar. Those legs could only belong to someone very tall. And they looked very much like those that had tripped her at the picnic and later taken over her bed.

No wonder she'd been bewitched.

This time when the light changed, she left rubber in her wake. At Kirby, she turned toward the Southwest Freeway and from there north. A check of her rearview mirror showed the Harley trailing close, easily keeping up even though she was already doing seventy.

Exhilaration from the thrill of a chase coursed through her, inappropriate but indisputable. "Hope the men in blue are patrolling somewhere else," she said, knocking on the burled wood dashboard as they approached the Oz-like towers of downtown.

Bentley slowed just enough to negotiate the spaghetti bowl interchange, but he edged closer still, practically nudging her bumper. Tires screaming, she veered onto the first exit ramp and zipped around several blocks before starting home. There was no sign of the man in black.

She drove sedately along side streets, shaking from her recklessness, unable to forget the image of the cycle or its rider. When she turned into her driveway, she spotted him waiting at the corner of the garage. She eased the Jag inside and armed herself for a confrontation. But as soon as she got out of the car, he touched his helmet in a two-fingered salute and roared off into the night.

He was the most maddening man she'd ever met! And, she admitted, the most fascinating. She doubted that even the flowers would be able to soothe her tonight.

Bentley set the alarm, then changed into a sheer cotton gown and removed her makeup, still debating whether she felt like tackling the flowers or not. It was nearly one and she should probably go to bed. Yes, she thought, turning back her comforter and crawling between the sheets. Sleep was the best remedy to exorcise the dark marauder from her mind.

Minutes ticked by, and she slowly drifted from drowsiness into a light sleep. The first peal of the phone jerked her upright, fighting the covers, fighting for breath. Her heart slammed mercilessly; her skin felt cold and clammy all over. She swallowed against the familiar nausea.

The nightmare couldn't be starting all over. Not here.

She'd come back to Houston to be safe. Never again would she allow a faceless voice to terrorize her, to make her sick with dread every time she stepped outside her home.

The phone continued its unrelenting attack on her sanity. As it always did. But this time, she wasn't going to cower in petrified silence. This time she would fight. With a shaky hand, she lifted the receiver. Listened. Prayed she could confront the voice without breaking.

"Bentley?"

"Reid!" One word was all she could manage before her voice cracked.

"Bentley, is that you? Are you all right?"

Oh, Reid!" Hearing herself whimper, she collapsed against the pillow, faint with relief. "Reid." She couldn't stop saying his name, as if it were some kind of talisman to hold the panic at bay. "Reid."

"Honey, what's the matter? Damn! Did I wake you? Did the phone scare you? I'm sorry, I didn't think. Damn!"

She bit her knuckles, afraid she was on the verge of either hysterical laughter or a crying fit. He kept talking to her in that soft, devastating voice, imploring her to tell him what was wrong. Oh, how she wanted to let it all pour out, to lean on him for comfort and reassurance.

But when she'd left New York, she had vowed to leave all that mess behind, too. Which meant never reprising that frightening period of her life. It represented a disturbing weakness in herself, one she did not want to expose to Reid. Where he was concerned, she needed every measure of strength at her command.

With such a forceful man, a woman continually ran the risk of losing herself in his dominance. Bentley was determined that no man would wield that kind of power over her. *So stop acting like a ninny and assert yourself.*

She opened her mouth to speak. All that came out was a muffled, "Uhhh."

"That does it. I'll be there in less than ten minutes. Don't worry, sweetheart, everything's gonna be okay."

_____ FIVE _____

The possibility of him seeing her like this galvanized Bentley and restored her voice. "No, no. You don't need to come here. I'm fine. Really," she insisted with false heartiness. Could he hear her inner tension as clearly as she did?

"You don't sound fine."

"I was asleep when the phone rang." True, as far as it went. "That's always a shock. You expect bad news, or something." Like your life being threatened in grisly detail. She shook her head to dispel the ghastly visual.

"I guess. But you still don't sound quite right. I think I'll come on over anyway and see for myself that you're okay."

"No, no," she repeated, more purposefully this time. "Just talk to me. That'll take my mind off . . . whatever."

"Did you have a good time at the wedding?"

Bentley closed her eyes. Apparently her ploy had worked. Now all she had to do was sound normal. "As a matter of fact, I did. Until afterward."

71

"Oh? Why is that?"

Surely he didn't think he'd fooled her with his late-evening appearance. "Your excuse had better be good," she said, without leveling a specific accusation.

"I only wanted to make sure you got home safely," he offered without hesitation. "Saturday nights are treacherous; a lady can never tell when she might need a protector."

He spoke with a drawl, the way he did when he said something outrageous. "You know what they say about chivalry, don't you?"

"No, but I'll bet I'm about to find out."

"Chivalry is a man's inclination to defend a woman against every man except himself." His laugh rang with pleasure, as if she'd paid him a compliment. Bentley pursed her lips to keep from laughing, too. How quickly he'd chased away the ghosts.

"I confess. You've found me out." He didn't attempt to hide his reason for following her. "I could live with the dancing, but the idea of you in another man's arms later gave me second thoughts."

She ought to give him an earful about jealousy and possessiveness and other male foibles. "Would a lecture do any good?" she asked, suspecting it would be wasted effort.

"Probably not, but if it'll make you feel better, go ahead. I'm willing to take my medicine like a big boy."

"I think I'll pass." The adrenaline was subsiding, leaving her weak and trembly. "Go back to what you were doing." She stretched out, unable to suppress a sigh.

"Are you still in bed?"

She tensed at his change of tone, and a different kind of weakness overtook her. "Why?"

"Never mind. I know you are. You're lying on that satin comforter that smells like your perfume. And wearing something sexy. If I were there with you, I'd run my hands all over you and both of us would be burning up."

Bentley's palm covered her heart, which had started racing again. He could seduce with nothing more than his voice. It had the texture of a lava flow and she felt its accompanying fire deep within her. She had to stop this, but while she struggled to find the words, he continued to ravish her senses.

"Every night since I slept in your bed, I've thought about you there. I remember the flowers, on a table in front of the window and the nightstand . . . even in your dressing room. Everything there is just like you, Bentley, beautiful and feminine and very, very seductive." He groaned. "Do you have any idea what this is doing to me?"

She gulped, knowing all too well. "Reid, I have to hang up." He had calmed her fear of the phone stalker; now his suggestive banter agitated her even more.

"No, don't. I'll stop if you'll talk to me a while longer." When she didn't reply right away, he said softly, "Please, Bentley, don't hang up yet."

She detected something she'd never heard before. He sounded a little desperate. "Reid, what is it? Are *you* all right?"

There was a moment's pause before he answered in a strained voice. "I'm all right. I'm just . . . lonely. I don't know why."

She sensed his reluctance to make the admission. Like most men, he no doubt saw it as a flaw. "It happens to all of us at times. It's late and you're probably tired. Why don't you get some rest?"

"I don't ever remember being lonely."

He sounded like a forlorn little boy. Bentley's heart melted. She needed to do something to console him, which was exceedingly foolish. She did it anyway. "Would you like to come over for brunch tomorrow?"

Again he hesitated. "Yes. I would."

The silence dragged on until she said, "About eleven?"

He repeated the time, almost as if he didn't believe the invitation was real. "Bentley, I know I've given you a rough time, but if you'll only bend a little, it'll get easier. We can work around the problems."

"I don't think now is the time to—"

"Please, let me finish. I've thought this over since last night. I want . . . no, I *need* to be with you. And I'm not talking about sex. You make me feel good, give me something to think about besides business, make me want what I've been missing."

Bentley's breath caught. "I understand," she said, only to realize she meant it. She realized, too, that she was edging one step closer to a very dangerous admission. "But if you don't let me get some sleep, you'll go hungry in the morning."

"Right. See you at eleven."

Too late, she had the nagging suspicion that he'd manipulated her. She was simply too tired to worry about it. "Till then."

"One last thing. Plan on going to New York with me next weekend."

He hung up before Bentley could blurt out that she never wanted to set foot in New York again. Her life might depend on it.

At ten-thirty Sunday morning, Reid prowled rest-

lessly among the downstairs ruins of his house. Excess
energy was a fact of life for him. Usually it didn't
affect him the way it was doing today. He'd made several circuits through the wreckage, evaluating all the
work needed to make the place livable. Maybe Bentley
had the right idea, and he should hire it done. Seeing
how she lived, he knew she'd never be content in a
place like this. She'd expect, and deserve, better.

Confounded by where his thoughts had led, he
stopped short. "What the devil?" This heat must be
addling his brain. Or else Bentley North had gotten to
him more than he realized. Living with a woman was
something he'd never thought about, and he wasn't sure
he was ready for it now.

Granted, he looked forward to being with her, matching wits with her, teasing her. He wanted to make love
to her. But picturing Bentley in his home had come out
of nowhere, an intriguing notion. And an unlikely one.

She was adamant that everything between them remain strictly professional. He could go along with that
while they were involved in business. After hours he
considered her fair game and he intended to use every
one of his finely honed hunting instincts. Patience was
one of many virtues he hadn't been blessed with, but
nobody could fault his tenacity. He'd gotten much of
what he wanted that way.

Reid locked the house and walked his motorcycle out
of the garage. He'd let both the license tag and inspec-
tion sticker expire on his car, and had a ticket from the
DPS to prove it. Could have been worse. He'd been
doing ninety on the interstate to Dallas, but the officer
had cited him for the lesser offenses in exchange for a
promise of a Titan winning season. Reid was a good
negotiator.

He stomped the Harley to life and made mental notes of all the details he had to take care of tomorrow. Mrs. T. had recently informed him he needed a keeper . . . or a wife. Said he left everything hanging fire unless it was business.

Except today. He hadn't thought about Maverick once. He'd been too occupied with Bentley, ticking off the seconds until he could see her again. Impatience overtook him and he gave the Harley its head.

Bentley bustled about the kitchen, consulting her cookbook and gathering ingredients to prepare brunch. Her last thought before falling asleep had been that by morning she'd regret issuing Reid the invitation. Instead, she caught herself checking the clock every few minutes, counting the time until eleven.

Last night's phone call had brought about a subtle shift in their relationship. Reid had unknowingly rescued her from night demons, and she had satisfied a corresponding need in him. She chose not to dwell on what that implied.

Remembering his comment about her breakfast room being cozy, she considered setting the dining table, then ruled it out. Too formal for just the two of them. Besides, there was a lot to be said for coziness.

"Oh, Lord. Don't start thinking like that or you'll be beyond redemption." She got busy arranging the bright-green placemats and napkins, pottery, and flatware. "It's only brunch, not candlelight and champagne."

At 10:55 Bentley's eyes were glued to the clock and she had a severe case of jitters. She even jumped when the doorbell rang. Why couldn't he be late? With a little more time she could have gotten herself calmed down. An inner voice chided, "Who are you kidding?"

"Mmm," he said when she opened the door. It sounded more like a growl. "You look good enough to—"

"I invited you to eat, but I'm not on the menu." She masked her urge to smile with a stern tone. "Behave yourself or you can get back on that hawg and go home."

"You know you wouldn't find me half as interesting if I behaved myself. A man has to keep on his toes if he wants to hold your attention."

He'd definitely captured her attention and she found him far too interesting. "I doubt if you ever behaved, even when you were a child."

"I'm sure my parents would agree with you."

She stood back so he could enter, then led him up the polished oak stairs to the main floor, acutely conscious of his nearness as his footsteps echoed close behind her. "Why don't you wait in the living room while I finish cooking? The *Post* is on the butler's tray."

He followed her. "I'd rather watch you," he said, crossing his arms over his chest and propping himself against the kitchen doorframe. "Somehow I never pictured you as the domestic type, but you look cute at the stove."

She wrinkled her nose and dropped two filets on the preheated grill. "Didn't anyone ever teach you it's hazardous to your health to mess with the cook?"

He reached over and grasped the strings on her frilly linen apron, tugging her toward him. "How can I resist messing when the cook looks and smells so tasty?"

His mustache tickled the back of her neck, making her shiver.

"Rule number two . . ." She forgot that rule and all the others when his hands framed her waist, then slid to her stomach and nestled her against his hips. "Reid, please . . ." Again her voice trailed off because she felt exactly what he'd meant her to—that his body was hungry for more than food.

"Just wanted you to know," he said, releasing her at once.

Bentley couldn't think of a single pithy comeback. To fill the breach, she made a great flurry of whisking egg yolks to add to the tarragon mixture of the béarnaise sauce she'd already started. After flipping the sizzling steaks with all the finesse of an experienced fry cook, she slapped toasted English muffins on two plates. Beside them, she placed an artful fan of raspberries and kiwi.

Reid sauntered over and picked up the cookbook. *Oh, no*! She'd meant to put it away before he got there. "*Breakfasts for Lovers*, huh?" His brows climbed; he gave her his best sly smile. "Sounds right to me."

"Don't get any ideas," she advised. "It's only a book." A gag gift from a friend who knew how rarely she cooked, especially breakfast.

"Honey, I've had ideas about you from day one, and well you know it. I'm just being a gentleman and biding my time . . . for a while longer." His expression bland, he studied the menu on the opened page. "Royal Wedding." Golden-brown eyes pinned her. "Is that what we're having?"

Gentleman, indeed! "Forget it," she said, snatching

the book and cramming it in an already-full drawer.
"Food's ready. Now sit down."

"Yes, ma'am." She heard laughter buried in his
voice.

Using hot pads, Bentley removed two au gratin
dishes from the oven and carried the steaming creamed
eggs to the table, where she placed the dishes in their
straw holders. Next she arranged the medium-rare filets
atop the English muffins and spooned sauce over them.
"Voilà," she announced presenting his plate with a
flourish.

She'd expected him to rave about her culinary exper-
tise. Instead, he rose like the gentleman he'd claimed
to be and pulled out her chair.

Her appetite vanished, swept away by the knowledge
that she had gone to extremes with the meal because
she wanted to impress him with her domestic skills. It
was not a flattering self-portrait.

Reid separated the hands she'd clasped in her lap,
and rubbed his thumb slowly over the top of one. "I'm
glad you invited me here." His hand stilled, covering
hers completely. "But you're having second thoughts,
aren't you?"

She nodded, unsure whether her apprehension was
visible or if he'd read her mind. At the moment, she
felt as though she were precariously balanced on a tight-
rope with no safety net below.

"Don't waste your time worrying about it. We both
know the ultimate outcome. Try to relax. I'm not going
to pounce on you." He grinned and carved a bite of
steak. "Yet."

Hunter's prey. That's what she felt like. "Why
doesn't that reassure me?" she asked, attempting to
revive her sense of humor.

"Don't know. Anyone can see how trustworthy I am."

As quickly as the unease had descended on her, it vanished. She laughed and admonished him to eat before his food got cold. Reid might have innumerable faults, but she did not doubt his trustworthiness. She had complete trust that he would do precisely what he promised. In which case, she was in for big trouble. And like Scarlett, she'd think about it tomorrow.

When they'd finished, he turned his chair to the side and stretched out his legs. "You're a good cook."

She shrugged, determined to mask her pleasure at the compliment. "My talents are limited. I can turn out a respectable meal now and then, but I don't care to make a habit of it. You were right, I'm not very domestic."

"That makes two of us. Several years ago, Mrs. T. badgered me until I put in the employees' cafeteria. It was her mission to see that I gave up fast food and ate three squares a day."

Bentley smiled at the idea of tiny Marian Tolliver fussing over six feet three inches of irascibility. "I think she's pretty fond of you. Maybe even protective."

"Yeah, but don't accuse her of being soft. She likes to maintain the illusion of toughness. Says it helps her screen out those who don't really need to talk to me."

"As I said, protective."

"Mmm. She can't decide which I need most, a keeper, mother, or wife. I guess she sort of tries to combine all three. I don't mind indulging her."

It went beyond a willingness to indulge. "You're pretty fond of her, too, aren't you?"

He nodded. "Mrs. T. was the first person I hired when I started the computer company, and she stuck with me. Put up with me and a lot of other hardships. I owe her.''

Loyalty. It was an old-fashioned concept, one that didn't play a part in most corporate management policies. But in the short time she'd worked at Maverick, she'd seen plenty of evidence of it, and it was a two-way street. Another reason why Reid would never fit into anyone else's pattern. Another reason to admire him. Every day she found more traits Reid and her stepfather shared in common. Traits a woman could love.

You're doing it again. "I'll just clear the table," she said briskly. "Wait for me in the living room. This won't take long."

Minutes later she walked into the dining room and around the fireplace that separated it from her living room. Reid had his nose buried in the sports section. " 'Stros are playing the Cards at one. Want to head out to the Dome and see a doubleheader?"

Bentley hadn't thought ahead to what they'd do after brunch, but logic dictated that Reid didn't mean to leave soon. If they were going to be together, she'd prefer having several thousand chaperons. Anyway, she loved sports and hadn't been to a game in the Astrodome in ages. "Sure, why not."

And so, with very little effort, he had her committed to spending the rest of the day with him.

Bentley cheered when the Astros won the first game, booed when they lost the second, and was hoarse from several hours of constant yelling. Afterward they went to Angelo's for seafood and stayed long past the meal.

"Tell me why you wanted to start your own computer company," Bentley asked between sips of Irish coffee.

"Ah. Are we finally beginning our getting-to-know-you phase?"

"Orion Computers was the forerunner of Maverick. It's natural that I'd be curious."

"So it's only the company you're interested in, not me?"

"According to you they're one and the same," she said, a bit too harshly.

He lifted one shoulder. "After I graduated I went to work for a computer company and right away decided I could build a better one." His wry smile turned into a grimace. "Occupational hazard. Probably at least half a dozen hotshots at Orion right now are saying the same thing."

"The difference is that you did it. How long did it take?"

"Building and testing the original model took about three years. I found out later that was the easy part. See, I had a good idea, but no money to manufacture or market it. That's when the real work began, and it took another year to line up financial backing before we could start production." He spread his arms in an all-encompassing gesture. "The rest, as they say, is history."

Quite an impressive one, too. The graph tracking Orion sales had climbed steadily upward right from the start, every CEO's fairy tale come to life.

"Why Houston?" she asked. "Why not Silicon Valley or Washington state or some other computer mecca?"

"I'd traveled a lot on business, been to a bunch of cities. Houston just appealed. It's presumptuous; its technique suits me. Other places, they'd give someone like me a hundred reasons why my scheme wouldn't work. Here, nobody would think of telling you anything is impossible.''

He sat forward, elbows on the table. ''The whole damn city shouldn't even be here. It's built on a swamp.''

Bentley laughed at his description of her hometown. ''You're right. It isn't beautiful, not always well mannered, but there's a spirit here that just won't quit.'' She could see why it appealed to Reid.

''Yeah, that says it all.'' He sent a silent signal to the waiter, terminating the discussion.

She wasn't ready to let him off so easily. She wanted the whole story, straight from the tycoon's mouth. Bill said the worst use a man could make of his success was to boast about it. Confident as he was, no one could accuse Reid of being a braggart. ''So, are computers still your main interest?''

''Nope. The computer market seems soft to me right now. Mainly I'm involved in major policy decisions. For everything else, I hire good people, tell them what I want done and leave them alone to do it. Once I've accomplished what I started out to do, the day-to-day operations bore me. That's why I'm always on the lookout for something different. New fields to conquer.''

''New ways of making money?'' For as long as she could remember, Bentley had known she'd been well provided for financially. But growing up in River Oaks, she'd also been exposed to plenty of people who, having made fortunes overnight, flaunted it in the most pretentious ways. Reid with his tumble-down house, littered pickup truck, and vintage motorcycle hardly qualified as pretentious.

''Money? Well, I guess I'm interested in it.'' His eyes took on a distant look, as if he were casting about for words. Then he smiled. "But I'm not motivated by it. I never do anything because I think it'll make a lot of money. That's what separates me from most business people. I don't let myself be ruled by the bottom line."

"Maverick," she said in a near-whisper. The corporation's name defined Reid perfectly. "If you lost it all tomorrow, it wouldn't matter, would it?"

"Of course not," he scoffed. "I got where I am because I'm not afraid to fail. If I do, I'll just start over with something new." He grinned disarmingly. "Make a million, lose a million. What does it count for in the grand scheme of things? I was just as happy when I had less than fifty dollars in my checking account as I am having . . . as I am now."

Inordinately pleased by his attitude, she felt the radiance of her own smile. He had passed the test.

Reid reached across the table to grasp her hand. "Can someone like you possibly understand that money really plays no role in my life? That I don't even think about it?"

"I understand much better than you imagine," she said softly. Nothing like having one's life in jeopardy to clarify what was truly important. "Believe me, I know."

He squeezed her hand. "We're a lot more alike than we appear to be, Bentley North. When you realize just how much, it's going to work in my favor."

She was afraid it already had. There were so many qualities she admired in Reid, many she tried to emulate. But he was so tough, so impervious to threats or weakness. She could never hope to match his strength. Knowing that, she had to do her best to keep him at a distance.

"I'm fascinated by your choice of the name Orion,"

"I'm fascinated by your choice of the name Orion," she said, sounding disgustingly like a perky cheerleader. "Are you a mythology buff?"

He shifted in his chair and studied the check with more attention than it deserved. When he looked up, it was with a challenge in his eye. "Just remember, you had to know. If you laugh, I'll make you sorry you asked."

Bentley's smile widened. "This must be good."

"It's my middle name."

"How spectacular!" she exclaimed, clapping her hands once. "I love it! So appropriate—the mighty hunter."

"You like it?" He was clearly surprised.

"Like it? I think it's wonderful. So it was your parents who were into mythology."

"My mother. All four baby Hunters got named for one of her favorite characters, and those myths were our bedtime stories. I even called my first puppy Sirius."

"And your father didn't object?"

Reid's burst of laughter drew glances from other diners. "My dad is a basketball coach. He didn't protest too much about Daphne, but he had quite a bit to say about my brothers and me. He swore Reid Orion, Miles Leander and Lane Biton were sissy names, and we'd all come to bad ends because of them."

Bentley commended the unknown Mrs. Hunter for her courage. "If you're any example, I guess she proved him wrong."

"Coach never admits to being wrong. He just quits harping on the issue and that's your way of knowing it's dead." He left some money on the table. "Ready?"

She was ready to leave the restaurant, but her appetite for information about Reid had merely been whetted. As she drove them back to her townhouse, she pushed for more.

Using a minimum of words, he told her about the floundering soft drink company he'd wanted to rescue because he'd liked the drink ever since he was a boy. But he credited an eccentric songwriter's catchy jingle and a clever national advertising strategy with saving the company from failure.

Impressed with the ad agency's work, he bought it, issuing only one directive. No boring commercials. A large manufacturer of sporting goods was acquired next. He liked all kinds of sports. So it was inevitable that when the Titans basketball franchise came up for sale, he was first in line.

"Which brings me around to next weekend," he said as they pulled into her garage.

Bentley got out of the car. All day, she'd purposely refrained from asking about the trip to New York. She wanted to postpone the inevitable as long as possible.

"A week from Tuesday is the basketball draft. The Titans won the lottery and we have first pick. We're going to take Lowell Hawkins." He came to join Bentley where she stood just outside the garage.

She nodded. The Titans first round draft choice was the sports world's worst-kept secret. "Skyhips," she said, using the seven-foot center's nickname.

"Right. He's going to form the nucleus of a championship team. I've hired one of the league's best coaches, and with some off-season trades and a good draft, we'll have a contender in no time."

Typical Hunter optimism. He wanted a winner and would stop at nothing to get it.

"How do I fit into this?" Hope and dread warred inside her.

"I want you there for the draft because you'll be negotiating Sky's contract."

Bentley exploded in a burst of activity. She threw her arms around Reid and kissed his cheek before dancing away excitedly. This was a plum assignment, better than anything she'd hoped for. "You really mean it?"

"Mmm." He came toward her. "If I'd known you would react this enthusiastically, I'd have told you a long time ago."

Her smile froze as he captured her in his arms. Her efforts to escape didn't faze him. "Now come here, Bentley. Show me how grateful you are."

SIX

Bentley's mouth dropped open as fury engulfed her. Did he believe for a second she'd submit to his flagrant attempt at blackmail?

"Save your indignation," he told her, before she could think of a stinging rebuff to his offensive suggestion. "I was only teasing, not threatening."

"Oh," she said, deflated because he'd stolen her thunder. "You ought to know better than to tease about this, Reid. Have you forgotten your promise not to hassle me?"

"You and I have a deal. I never make an agreement I can't honor. As long as you see me away from the office, I won't pressure you while you're working. I can live with that, though I don't care much for charades. Just be sure you appreciate that not many people slip bargains like this one past me."

Bentley looked up into his eyes, detecting a trace of amusement. Wresting even a small concession from him gave her an inordinate amount of pleasure. "Are you saying I belong to the privileged few?"

"There aren't even a few. Only you, so enjoy it."
He braced one hand on the garage and leaned toward
her, close, but not touching. "Now, can I finish the
business with my employee so I can collect a good-
night kiss from my woman?"

His woman! Bentley's breath caught at the posessive-
ness of the word. Why couldn't she find her voice and
tell him that she would never be any man's *woman*?
Why did she want him to forget business, go ahead and
collect his kiss? Even more disturbing, why did she
hope he wouldn't settle for only a kiss?

As if his thoughts mirrored her own, Reid said,
"Aw, hell. Forget business until tomorrow. I've suffered all day. I want the kiss."

She stood unwavering, waiting for him to take what
he wanted and give her what she needed.

"Do you know what happens now, Bentley? I'm
not your boss. I'm Reid, the man who wants you."

Her mouth was so dry she couldn't speak, could only
nod understanding. He placed his other hand on the
garage, penning her, leaving no room to retreat. The
bricks imprinted her bare back, but his hard contours
pressing her into the cool abrasion were just as unyielding. Trapped between two immovable objects, she
didn't hesitate before choosing Reid's warmth.

His lips were so near hers that she felt the inviting
warmth of his breath, the elusive brush of his mustache.
"Tell me what you want right now."

"Your mouth on mine. Hard."

He made a very masculine sound deep in his throat
and fused their lips. Heat and hunger exploded inside
her, driving her to touch him everywhere—arms, shoulders, face. She embraced him fully, massaging the muscles of his back, learning that her hands could make

them ripple and undulate. Swept up in her own power, she wanted to unleash the full force of Reid's potent masculinity.

He parted her lips, tasting, taking time to savor the pleasure of each lazy thrust. His tongue, at first a gentle invader, grew bolder, penetrating again and again, so brazen she felt as if she were surrendering more than just her mouth. Her tongue met his, seduced by the primitive, pulsing rhythm that substituted for the ultimate joining.

He was a man who knew what he wanted, and he was very thorough about taking it. Even if it was only one kiss. Bentley had never realized that a single kiss could last so long, inspire such need, promise so much. Reid's withdrawal left her bereft and trembling until the fluid heat of his words washed over her, drawing her back from the brink.

"Is this the night? Are you going to let me take you to bed? Will you make love to me as passionately as I mean to love you?"

His voice, thick with desire, weakened her. Unsure that her legs would hold her up, she leaned into his strength and buried her face in the soft cotton of his shirt. *No*, her logical self protested. But her body screamed *yes*.

"Feel us. We're both on fire. I want to make you even hotter."

She shuddered, restless and feverish and yearning. Her willpower at low ebb, she could barely shake her head in refusal. "I can't let you, Reid. I . . ." Bentley knew now that the question was no longer *if* it would happen, but how long she could forestall her fate. "Not yet."

"Then I've got to get out of here." He stepped back.

"Do you understand? I can't touch you or kiss you again because I won't be able to stop." He groaned and swiped a hand over his face. "Lord, this is pure agony. I ache."

Bentley pressed her fingers to her lips, holding back the words that would stop him from leaving. She watched him mount the Harley and stomp it to life, a dark outline against the ghostly moon. The machine rumbled and bucked as he snapped the chin strap of his helmet and tore off into the night.

She heard the powerful engine wind up when he reached the street. "Please be careful," she whispered, unable to bear the thought of anything happening to Reid.

She was falling in love with him.

The following week fulfilled Bentley's every expectation about what working at Maverick would be like. First thing Monday morning Reid had summoned her to his office for a briefing on her next assignment. Feeling defenseless after her startling admission of the night before, she dreaded facing him. Her fears had proved unfounded. He was all business, and had given her what she'd been waiting for, work she could sink her teeth into.

One of the things she most enjoyed about her profession was playing detective. It was absorbing to take a case which had few or no precedents and prepare a defense based on her own research. The week flew by because she was totally immersed in moving her puzzle pieces into place.

A group of local fans, disgruntled that the Titans consistently finished at the bottom of their division, had filed suit against the franchise. They claimed buying tickets to a professional basketball game constituted a contract and that the team's repeated losses should be considered breach of contract.

Reid had railed against having to dignify such a charge and condemned the attorneys who'd filed the suit, calling them shysters. Bentley confidently assured him it was no more than a nuisance that could be easily handled. After thorough research of all possibilities, she prepared a motion to dismiss, claiming insufficient grounds for action. With the backlog in Harris County, she felt sure no judge would deem the case worthy of the court's time, and it would be tossed out.

With that project completed, she had to face facts. She'd purposely put off thinking about the New York trip, knowing it would send her into a tailspin if she dwelled on it. Much as she feared going there, she saw no alternative.

Reid had handed her a boon when he'd decided to entrust her with negotiating the superstar's contract. He'd given her the perfect vehicle to ensure her success at Maverick, as well as a way to escape from his direct supervision. It was an opportunity she had to seize, a job she had to do well.

There had been a time in her life when Bentley would have been jubilant at the chance to take New York by storm, show them what she was made of. All that changed once she became a prisoner of shadows trailing her and phone calls that turned the darkness into a living hell.

But she had to go. And perhaps in doing so she could confront her fears and conquer them for good.

Saturday afternoon when they arrived at their hotel, Bentley suffered through a few apprehensive minutes.

The closer they'd come to Manhattan the edgier she'd grown, and finding out she would be sharing a suite with Reid did nothing to allay her anxiety.

She had seen very little of him during the previous week and he had spent the entire flight working out of his briefcase. To his credit, he'd adhered to his pledge to treat her like any other employee while they were working. Bentley was grateful for his forbearance; she didn't need any additional pressure on her from Reid.

Perversely, she resented him for being able to act as though Sunday night had never happened. He didn't look at her like a woman he'd ravished with his kisses and promises of passionate lovemaking. While she couldn't look at him at all without remembering. Unfair, she thought, but then, she had been at a disadvantage with Reid from the beginning.

The suite had two bedrooms and baths, separated by a large parlor and a dining area large enough to entertain guests. There was no danger that they'd be tripping over each other. Indeed, Reid immediately claimed the phone, making what she could tell were business calls.

Feeling superfluous, she went into her room and started unpacking. A short time later, he rapped on her half-open door.

"Bentley, I've got meetings so you're on your own. Tomorrow at one, I'll need you here, probably for the rest of the day and through dinner. Then Monday, we'll be tied up all day." He started to leave, but tacked on an afterthought. "Keep Monday night free, too, just in case." Without waiting for her confirmation, he vanished.

Bentley glowered at the empty doorway, then gave it an impudent salute. "Yes, sir, Mr. Hunter. Your wish is my command." The door to the hall clicked shut in the middle of her childish outburst, but she felt better even if he had missed it. The bravura soon deserted her.

She was on her own. In New York. Her hands started to shake, her stomach churned.

"Don't do this," she ordered herself. "Don't let that slimy creep do this *to* you." Vowing not to hole up like a fugitive, she pounced on the phone and within minutes had scheduled drinks at the hotel with one group of friends and dinner at Mario's with another. Her cousin Ryan would meet her for breakfast in the hotel's coffee shop tomorrow morning.

"How's that for being on my own, boss?" she asked the empty suite, then choked out a brittle, self-deprecating laugh. Reid certainly wasn't worried about leaving her alone and defenseless in the big city. Of course, he had no way of knowing there was just cause for concern.

The next morning Bentley woke from a fitful sleep, feeling grouchy for no particular reason. The phone hadn't rung once, nor had anything else disturbed her. These days she was a light enough sleeper that she'd have heard Reid's key in the door. Was the fact that she hadn't heard it at all responsible for her grouchiness?

"You're really losing it," she chastened herself, diving into the shower. "None of your business where he spent the night. You'd be better off all around if he's taken up with some gold digger who'll keep him occupied and out of your hair."

Liar, her conscience taunted. And a jealous one at that.

She'd gotten her rampant emotions under control by ten o'clock when she met Ryan in the lobby. Wearing a spring-green silk suit, Irish linen blouse, and a coordinating wide-brimmed hat made her feel chic and in charge.

"Hello, cousin," he said, giving her an affectionate peck on the cheek. "You're looking cool and efficient this morning."

"As do you." She eyed his pleated white slacks and navy blazer. "Taken up yachting, have you?"

"Image, all image," he informed her as they strolled into the restaurant. "That's the first thing we advertising flacks learn. What you *think* you see is what you get."

They laughed and accepted menus from the hostess. "So, how are you adjusting to life back in the provinces?"

"Spare me your New York chauvinist routine, Ry. There is life west of the Hudson."

"Or some semblance thereof. But don't you miss all this?" He gave a magnanimous gesture.

Like the rest of her family, Ryan didn't know the real reason she'd abandoned the city. "Not in the least," she said vehemently. "I couldn't get away soon enough."

Ryan frowned at her sharpness, and she saw questions forming. Since she didn't want to elaborate, Bentley forced a smile and said, "It was time for a change, that's all."

"Ah, yes. Your new job. Is the famous Renegade as bold and brash as he appears?"

"More so," she admitted. In more ways than even Ryan could imagine.

"But you can . . . manage him?"

She nodded and told him a bald-faced lie. "Of

course." If she was in any way managing Reid, it was at his sufferance and temporary at best.

"Of course. Not a man alive you can't handle, yew sweet thang," he drawled in a ludicrous Texas accent he'd never had when he lived there. "Not even a maverick like Hunter. Right?"

Bentley started to agree, but the words died unspoken when a movement at the doorway caught her eye. Like an actor in a play, the subject of their discussion hovered in the wings, waiting to make his entrance.

Reid waved aside the hostess, indicating he would join Bentley and Ryan. When he started in their direction, she groaned. His gaze locked on hers and never deviated the entire time it took him to cross the room.

He was wearing gray slacks and a pinstriped shirt, not the navy suit she'd last seen him in, proving he had been back to the suite sometime.

As he neared their table, Bentley made herself face Ryan, as if she could turn Reid into a figment of her imagination by not looking at him.

The figment swooped down and took her mouth in a kiss that was short, but undeniably territorial. "Sorry I had to leave before you woke up, honey."

She feigned a cough that turned into a giggle. Men and their macho posturing were sometimes so incredibly transparent, so unbelievably boyish. Or was that *boorish*?

And Ryan didn't acquit himself any more favorably than Reid. He jumped up and seized the taller man's hand with an alacrity that would have been embarrassing had it not been so laughable.

"I'm Ryan Elliott, Mr. Hunter. Bentley's cousin."

Couldn't he have played along a while longer so she could watch Reid flex his masculine ego? It would have been interesting to witness him wiggle his way out of that. But Ry's primary aim had been protecting his handsome hide. Reid's demeanor had been quite ominous when he arrived.

Looking at them now, one would think they were old pals. They rattled on, ignoring her as if she'd suddenly become invisible. Bentley's fingers gripped the stem of her goblet and she considered dumping ice water in their laps.

For the next hour, she ate and drank and devised more elaborate forms of revenge. She'd make sure that turncoat Ryan paid dearly for all those childhood stories he told on her, the ones Reid seemed to find so entertaining.

But in the end, the men stood and shook hands again. She realized she'd tuned them out and had no idea what Reid meant when he said, "Send me that work we talked about and I'll get back in touch with you."

Ryan thanked him, winked at Bentley, and left her gaping long after he'd made a debonair exit.

"Close your mouth," Reid ordered. "It's damned tempting when you look like that.

"For once . . . she did . . . what I told her," Reid panted, his words punctuated by noisy gulps of air, echoed by his pounding feet. He replayed the preceding day's events which had led him to his present miserable circumstances.

Actually, Bentley had done everything he'd told her this trip, and done it well. From yesterday morning in the coffee shop right up until he'd sent her off to bed at one-thirty this morning, she'd followed orders without question.

"Uhh," he huffed, speeding up to overtake a weaving derelict. They had endured twelve hours of continuous meetings, and she had impressed him with her intelligence and legal ability. Of course, that was what he paid her for, but he still enjoyed seeing her in action.

She never raised her voice or became strident and argumentative. Neither did she rely on feminine wiles to wheedle or cajole. But she never backed down. *That* he liked.

He exhaled a breathy chuckle. She'd had those hard-nosed cable-TV executives dancing to her tune, and they'd never even heard the music. She'd gotten them to agree to some very beneficial terms for the broadcast rights to Titan games, terms that would net Reid's corporation a lot of money.

He drove a hard bargain himself, but his technique was generally to hammer away at his opponents until they caved in. Bentley used finesse and an inherent facility for dealing with people that he'd never perfect if he tried for a century. No, that wasn't his way, but he respected it and the woman who practiced it so skillfully.

The lady was savvy as well as beautiful. The idea that he'd fallen in love with her satisfied him as much as any success he'd ever achieved. Maybe more.

"Well, hell!" He narrowly missed taking a headlong dive after tripping over his own feet. Reid Hunter in love? Possible? "Hell, yes." There wasn't any doubt. It came to him in a flash, like all his other brainstorms. And, as always, he was positive it was right. Now all he had to do was convince Bentley.

He had wanted and gone after a great deal in his life, but no woman had ever fallen into the category of things he'd desired intensely enough to pursue with the dedication he devoted to other projects. He could do it, though. And the prize would be worth any amount of effort.

Reid knew one thing for sure. Bentley North was the only thing on earth that could drive him to jog . . . through Central Park no less. At three o'clock in the morning. . . .

Bentley was dimly aware that it was three-thirty A.M. Was she awake or did that fact play some part in a dream? She stirred, seeking to evade the chilly fog that swirled around her, making it difficult to breathe. The fog turned colder and thickened. From a distance she heard her own broken gasps, felt the fog suffocating her.

Reality or nightmare?

The phone jangled, a macabre reality because she recognized the visceral twisting in the pit of her stomach and what it portended.

The ringing continued, piercing her with its grotesque summons. If she didn't pick it up, the death knell would go on and on—forever—until it claimed her sanity. He knew she was there. He knew. He knew. He knew. And her tormentor never gave up.

Slowly she carried the receiver to her ear, as if a sinister magnet drew it there against her will. He opened with the same words he'd always used. "Bentley Brighton North?" His voice was so cold, so diabolic he could make even a name sound profane.

"Leave me alone, you animal. You can't get away with this." *But who will stop him*? "I won't stand for you hounding me this way. What do you want from me?"

He told her, in lurid detail, and Bentley heard herself

shriek, "No!" then sob, "No. What kind of ghoul are you?"

She found out precisely what kind when he described what he had done to several other victims, people he said who'd displeased him *less* than Bentley had.

Hysteria clawed at her. She fought to stem it, knowing that this piece of subhuman garbage would relish her agony. But he'd driven her to the edge of an abyss and she had to take a stand. "Leave me alone or I'll kill you before you can get to me. Do you hear me? I'll kill you!"

Her whole body convulsing, she collapsed on the bed, clutching the receiver, sobbing uncontrollably.

The bedroom door crashed open. Bentley screamed. Terror immobilized her. She curled into herself, certain her executioner had been miraculously transported and she would have to confront him face-to-face before he slowly, pervertedly made good on every single one of his threats.

"Bentley?"

Her head snapped up. She saw Reid filling the doorway, clad only in a towel knotted at his waist, eyes ablaze like an avenging warrior. "What the hell is going on?"

Her mouth worked silently, too dry to form words. She shook her head and fumbled to conceal the phone in the bedding. Using her palm, she attempted to dry her face. "N-nothing. You have to g-get out of here." She could not allow him to see her so incapacitated by fear.

Reid stormed over and wrenched the phone from her frozen fingers. "I don't know who you are," he snarled into the mouthpiece, "but you've made a *big* mistake.

Bother her again and you'll find out just how big." He hung up with enough force to shatter the plastic.

Hands on his hips, he glared down at her. "Who was it?" he demanded starkly.

"I . . . I don't know."

"Try again, North. I'm not buying."

She hugged a pillow to her chest and said, "I *don't* know who it is." His silence was as articulate as a demand. "That is, not exactly."

"Don't tell me you don't know something about him. He obviously knows enough details about you to scare you spitless."

When she continued to resist, he said in a too-quiet voice, "I heard most of the filth that vermin threatened you with. Talk like that would scare anybody."

"You heard?" Bentley buried her face in the pillow. She hadn't imagined her plight could get worse. But now, Reid was involved and he wouldn't be easily placated.

"I'd just stepped out of the shower when the phone rang." He glanced down at the towel. "Right away I picked up to see if it might be the call I'd placed to Scotland. Imagine my surprise."

"This is New York," she reminded him, deciding to take one more stab at evasion. "All kinds of crazies. The city never sleeps. Sooner or later that kind of thing is bound to catch up with all of us."

"Uh huh. And that particular weirdo has caught up with you lots of times, hasn't he? He knows what you look like, where you lived, and where you shop for underwear." He sat on the edge of the bed. "That's just a little too close for your average crazy, isn't it, Bentley?"

"Yes," she whispered, hugging the pillow more tightly.

He disentangled her from the pillow, giving her his hands to cling to. "So what's this all about? Who's behind it?"

"I can't prove anything."

"I don't need proof. I need details. Start at the beginning."

Bentley gazed into his eyes for a long time and finally came to the conclusion that they'd reached a turning point. "It began when I was assigned to prosecute a case here. A man—Bart Moreland—was accused of putting out a contract hit on one of his . . . competitors."

Reid's fingers tightened on hers. "Are we talking organized crime?"

"Well, again there's no evidence you can take to court against him on that charge. Only suspicions. The tax people have looked at him numerous times, but he always comes out pure as virgin snow. Only legitimate businesses with internal audits and financial statements by a reputable firm."

"So you were trying him on murder for hire?"

"No, my case was bribery and jury fixing. Seems that someone—of course Mr. Moreland had no idea who—tried to buy some insurance that justice would be done. Justice as they saw it."

Reid cursed. "Then the calls started when you went to trial?"

"Almost to the day." She shivered at the memory of how insidiously the caller had taken over her life. "At first they were more like your generic threats, vaguely menacing, but not directed specifically at me."

Reid shifted so that he could wrap one arm around

her shoulders. "They obviously degenerated into something worse."

"Yes, much worse. Eventually he would call every night, and every night his descriptions would get more personal and more brutal."

"Why didn't you get an unlisted number? Why didn't they tap your line and catch the bastard?"

"I wanted to . . . encourage him to a certain extent."

"You set yourself up as bait?" he shouted, shaking her slightly. "Damn, Bentley, what made you take a chance like that? Didn't you stop to think how dangerous that was?"

"We . . . I thought if I could string him along he'd say or do something incriminating, and we could nail him."

"But it didn't work. He's still out there tyrannizing you at will." His thumb and forefinger repeatedly shaped his mustache, a habit he reserved for contemplation. "You quit your job and left New York because of this, didn't you? All that talk in the interview about needing a change was just a smoke screen."

She was stunned by his perceptive guess. "I *did* need a change. The trial dragged on and that voice night after night. . . ."

"It finally got to you," he finished. "You started having trouble sleeping, and you examined every face you saw as a possible murderer." He tipped up her chin so he could see her face. "You *believed* he was going to kill you, didn't you?"

"Yes! Yes!" Great tremors rocked her body. "He told me he would, over and over." Her voice rose until it was almost a wail. "Oh, Reid. I was so afraid. Petrified. And I hated knowing that I was such a coward.

I'd always thought I was strong and brave. But that taught me I'm not. I'm weak and wimpy, and it just makes me furious.''

She dissolved into another fit of tears, more from self-disgust than fear. Now Reid would see her as she really was, with all her defenses shattered. A man like that would either pity her or take advantage. She couldn't bear the thought.

His other arm came around her, holding her hard against him, and he chuckled. "Such talk. The Bentley North I know *is* strong and brave. Nothing wimpy about her.''

"But—''

He hushed her with a kiss, very light, very undemanding. "Hey, it takes a strong, brave woman to bargain with me. I know one when I see her.''

It was sweet of him to console her like this, and his mere presence had again calmed her near-delirium. It was almost too much. She had admired his strength all along. That he could combine it with tenderness and concern made him close to irresistible.

"Listen to me, Bentley, and have faith in what I'm saying. That man will never get close to you. Not here. Not anywhere. I can make sure of it.''

A man who'd use his strength on behalf of a woman, not against her, was a formidable ally. She stirred in his embrace. "But Reid, you can't imagine how monstrous these characters are. They'll stop at nothing, not even murder. They don't think like normal people. They're beyond reason, beyond humanity. And beyond the reach of the legal system.''

She shook her head, feeling as if she'd used up all her energy fighting them. And what had she gained? "They are invincible.''

"Will you believe that I will never let them hurt you?"

His hands were heavy and insistent on her, and she wracked her brain for some reason why he was so bent on protecting her, on having her acknowledge not only his ability, but his right to do so.

In that moment of absolute vulnerability, she was willing to grant him anything. "I want to believe."

"Then do it." He rearranged them so that they were reclining with her back nestled against his front and both his arms encircling her. She felt very safe. And he felt very warm. "Reid?"

"Shh, I'm just going to hold you for a while. It'll be okay. I promise. Relax."

She did, a little, mainly because Reid had promised her it would be okay. From somewhere in the recesses of her battered consciousness, she understood that his promises were as precious as solid gold. A person could trust them, trust him to honor them.

Secured in his hold, Bentley at last was able to sleep again. Though she woke often, Reid was always there to reassure her that she was safe. And each time he repeated, "I'll take care of it for you. Believe me."

She did.

SEVEN

Bentley had set the alarm for seven, and when she woke, Reid was no longer holding her. Considering the sheer terror that had ravaged her during the night, she felt remarkably well rested and composed. After every other previous episode, she'd awakened feeling like she had been bludgeoned. It annoyed her to think Reid might be responsible for her peace of mind. It gave him still more power over her.

Pushing the covers aside, she sat up, and for the first time realized he had seen her in a very low-cut pink silk gown. Feather-light, it took up so little space in a suitcase that she always packed it when she traveled. If he'd noticed at all, he hadn't made a big deal of it.

She had just scooped up the matching robe when Reid spoke to her from outside the door. "Bentley, please be ready by a quarter to nine. I've scheduled a press conference and I want you to appear with me."

"No problem," she called out on her way to the bathroom. "I'll be ready." Reporters didn't daunt her and she'd learned to use a microphone in her face to maximum advantage. Public opinion was a powerful weapon.

Reid didn't court notoriety; he was by no means a media hound. But he wasn't above using them if doing so suited his purposes. And they were eager to oblige, knowing that if the Renegade said something, it would be newsworthy.

She assumed his announcement had to do with an eleventh-hour trade coup the Titans had pulled off. There were always rumors afloat in the sports world, and one in particular had been circulating for the past week. What if the Houston franchise had managed to lure a certain Chicago megastar into the fold? Would she be in a position to negotiate *two* big-name contracts?

Bentley chose her outfit with the camera in mind. A light-gray suit to match her eyes. The palest of pink blouses, to flatter her complexion. And slightly higher than normal gray pumps to give her presence.

She needn't have bothered, she saw later when they entered a large meeting room in the hotel. Reid commanded center stage. No one was imposing enough to overshadow him.

Both his hands gripped the microphone, as if he intended to throttle it. Bentley didn't miss the irony. This was the way he did business . . . and everything else.

"You may be wondering why I've called you all here."

The assemblage laughed, as if on cue.

"What I have to tell you is not funny." His audience sobered immediately. A hush prevailed. "This is about justice. And those who believe they are above it."

Notebooks and tape recorders were brandished like

magic wands. Bentley snapped to attention, her sixth sense telling her that what Reid was about to say had nothing to do with basketball.

"Most of you know I prefer action to words. But there are times when a few words in the right ear will do the job. I'm counting on this being one of those times."

He motioned for Bentley to join him. Heart pumping, she walked to stand beside him. "For those of you who don't recognize her, this is Bentley North. She works for Maverick Enterprises now, but before that she served as a prosecutor here in Manhattan."

Pens and cameras dutifully poised, the reporters waited. "To make a long story short, her life has been threatened—viciously—because she recognizes the difference between right and wrong, and believes that those who disregard it should pay for their crimes."

Bentley wanted to vanish. No, better that she scream at him to not expose her secret. But he did, and she stood there mute, granting him the right. He related a capsule version of her victimization. Without naming names, he summarized the story in chilling detail.

He finished with the admonition, "If anything happens to her, I don't care if it's an ankle sprain, I'm damned well going to wonder what caused it. And when I catch up with whoever's responsible, they will answer to me. Check the record or look in your files. It'll be easy to put two and two together and come up with your own conclusions."

Bentley strove to maintain a serene facade, while inside she was writhing. How dare he presume so much! She could envision the sort of rampant speculation this would cause. She'd be the subject of gossip and innuendo. Her effectiveness on the job would suffer. Damn him!

But you aren't as afraid this morning, her inner voice reminded, and she had to admit that was true. Clichéd as it sounded, sharing the burden had lightened it. As well as strengthening the bond between her and Reid.

Reid looked down at her, then at his audience. "That's all I intend to say on this subject. Ever. Thanks for listening. I appreciate your time."

They were shielded by a podium. No one could see his hand locked firmly around her waist, squeezing. But Bentley could feel it. And she pondered the ramifications of that protective, possessive form of claim-staking.

Bentley poured a healthy dose of Bill's favorite bourbon into an ice-filled glass and handed it to him.

"B.B., your mother's plumb hurt that you didn't tell us about that business in New York. So am I, for that matter." He shook his head and eased his chunky frame into one of her padded iron patio chairs. "And to think we heard the gory details on cable TV news. We should have known."

"Believe me, you weren't any more shocked when Reid went public with it than I was. I'm sorry you found out the way you did, but I stick by my decision not to tell the two of you, or anybody else. I knew how upset you'd be."

"Damn right we would!"

Bentley stretched out on a lounger. "I couldn't see what worrying you would accomplish. After all, it isn't as if you could have done anything about it."

Bill swizzled the drink with his forefinger before

downing a swallow. "Hunter didn't have any trouble stepping in and doing something, did he?"

She tipped her head and raised both brows. "Reid tends to be action oriented." A gross understatement. "He sort of forced me to tell all, and first thing the next morning we were making headlines."

Her stepfather set his drink on a small glass-topped table. "You know, after Tori got over the initial shock of hearing about those threats to her baby girl, she told me she didn't think you'd be bothered from now on, not with Hunter looking after you."

Given her mother's proclivity for romanticizing, Bentley knew she'd better put a damper on any notions Victoria might be harboring on that front. She wasn't yet comfortable enough with the depth of her feelings for Reid to confess them, not even to him. Especially not to him. "He doesn't take kindly to anybody harassing his employees." She stressed the last word.

"Tori also said, didn't the two of you make a fine-looking couple? Him so big and dark and fierce, you so fair and pretty."

"Oh, Bill," she said, rolling her eyes. "Doesn't she ever give up? She looks for romance between me and any male in reasonable proximity."

"Well, if that's the criteria, she's got a live one in Hunter. He made it clear in front of all those reporters that he is personally overseeing your well-being."

Bentley blushed, her initial embarrassment and consternation returning. She'd just known that everyone would read between the lines of Reid's bold statement. "I think Mother, and probably lots of other people, misinterpreted what he said. I just work for him and he's protective of his people by nature."

Bill nodded. "I can identify with that." He sat quietly for a few seconds, contemplating his drink. "So the job is all you thought it would be?"

She relaxed, relieved that he wasn't pursuing the personal connection between her and Reid. "Working at Maverick is like being in the middle of a whirlwind; there's always something happening. You feel this constant hum of energy and excitement. And Reid is the vortex, where the energy and excitement is most intense."

"Sounds like you've joined his fan club," Bill said gruffly. "Never known you to be one for hero worship."

"Hardly hero worship. The man has several glaring flaws." Which were more than counterbalanced by his admirable traits. "Still, I can't deny the positive effect he has on everybody who works for him."

She didn't want to remind Bill of her choice of Maverick over Willco, but she wanted him to see that she was happy with it. "It's the perfect job for me."

"I understand, hon. Really. It's clear that Hunter enjoys what he does, and he has an uncanny instinct for business. His company is not merely a job and I understand that, too. When I was younger, I felt the same way."

He sighed heavily and Bentley was again struck by how his attitude toward Willco had changed. His loss of enthusiasm was dramatic. "How are things going?"

Bill drained the glass in several swallows, then wiped his mouth with his palm. "What's got me concerned right now is our stock. It's been undervalued for quite a while, which isn't all that strange in today's market. But all of a sudden it's started trading like crazy and the price is going up. I don't like the signs."

Bentley didn't, either. A queasy sensation settled in her stomach. "Does this sound like a takeover?"

He levered himself up and walked over to stand at the balcony railing. "Probably not. Guess I'm just spooked by what happened to Sam Tankersley. He had to give up and let one of the big boys take his company."

She swiveled to face her stepfather. Bill and Sam had started out in the oil business at the same time and had been close friends for years. "I didn't know. I've stayed so wrapped up in my own work that I haven't paid attention to what's been going on. Sam must be crushed."

"He's taken it pretty hard, all right. Things've come to a sorry state when a man has no say in what happens to him."

Bentley couldn't shake the feeling that Bill wasn't referring only to Sam. She searched for the appropriate words with which she might reassure him that he was safe from the same fate. The words eluded her.

"What do you mean, he's not ready to sign?" Reid bellowed.

Bentley jerked the receiver away from her abused ear, grateful that he was in Seattle, separated from her by several thousand miles. For the past three days they'd held this same conversation with only minor variations. "I mean exactly what I said. I spoke with Lowell's mother today. He's fishing in the Ozarks and can't be reached."

His curses were articulate and imaginative, barometers of his frustrated need to get Skyhips's contract sewn up.

"It's physically impossible for me to talk terms with him when not even Mrs. Hawkins knows where he is."

"Then why aren't you up there trying to find him?"

Bentley made a face at the phone. "Probably because I'd have to search about forty thousand square miles. Even someone seven feet tall would be difficult to locate given that much territory." Her beleaguered ear found out he was in no mood for droll humor.

Bentley could hear a steady rat-a-tat and pictured Reid attacking something with a pen. "North, this is a loose end. I've no time for it. I have given you carte blanche with a pile of money and all I expect in return is a little piece of paper with a name on it. Is that so much to ask?"

"Not at all," she said, immune to his injured-party act. "I guarantee you'll have the paper and the name . . . but not for a few days."

There was a pause, followed by an exasperated sigh. "I'll hold you to that," he barked in his end-of-discussion voice. The dial tone blared in her ear before Bentley could finagle some extra time.

She depressed the button and punched out a series of numbers that were inscribed in her memory from numerous repetitions. The call followed the same pattern as all her prior ones. Skyhips Hawkins still could not be reached.

This was not a good time for Bentley to be having problems with her most crucial assignment. Following the basketball draft, she had returned from New York to work with Titan executives on the salary, bonus, and benefit packages the team planned to offer Sky, as well as their other draft choices. How could she have guessed the elusive superstar would take off on an odyssey and leave her stranded for weeks?

Reid had promptly left town again, initiating his routine of phone intimidation. Bentley didn't want to think about it, but her first six weeks at Maverick were up this Friday. So far she hadn't accomplished anything spectacular, at least not something significant enough to impress her boss and get her off probation.

Not so long ago she'd been prepared to tell Reid Hunter to take a hike and take his job along with him. Now it seemed imperative that she keep both. He wasn't an easy man to work for. There was no ease in him. Probably never would be.

Yet she couldn't imagine how ordinary and uninspiring her life would be without Reid. And she could no longer shy from the truth: She had fallen one hundred percent, head over heels in love with him.

Good news arrived just in the nick of time Thursday morning. Sky finally returned Bentley's call and she was able to persuade him to hop a plane that very afternoon and fly to Houston. She had it in the back of her mind to meet his flight and spirit him away for a working holiday at her godmother's ranch in the hill country.

She knew hers was an unorthodox way of handling the situation, but she wanted to confer with Sky in a stress-free setting, without Reid or the media swarming all over them. Bentley considered it a good omen when they managed to get away from Houston without being discovered.

All the way over, Sky chatted excitedly about his first visit to a real Texas ranch. Despite his extraordinary talent in basketball and the three-point-six average he'd carried through engineering school, Lowell Hawkins struck her as rather naive. Not unintelligent, certainly, just open and without guile. He was the type of young man every female would want to mother.

There'd be no shortage of candidates who'd want to do more than that. He was already famous, would very soon be rich, and was cute as a puppy, to boot. A dynamite package.

"Don't be overwhelmed by Letty," she warned him as they neared the final turn in the ranch road. "She has a fondness for the outrageous."

Leticia Hamilton's name was the only prim thing about her, which was why no one ever called her by it. To Bentley, she'd always been Aunt Letty even though they weren't related. It had been almost two years since she'd seen the older woman, and she was looking forward to the reunion.

"About time you moved back where you belong, missy," Letty scolded as soon as they'd gotten out of the car. After she and Bentley exchanged a long hug, she turned to Sky, making a big production out of assessing all eighty-four inches of him. "You sure you ain't Texan, boy? Didn't think they grew 'em this big anywhere else."

"Couldn't you restrain yourself long enough to be introduced, Auntie? Say hello to Lowell Hawkins."

Letty reached up and pumped his hand, her only concession to propriety. "You got any other name, son? Lowell sounds kind of prissy to me, not that you can help what somebody else named you."

"Skyhips is my nickname," he blurted out, obviously nonplussed by her candor.

Letty spoke with more authority than anyone who stood barely five feet had a right to. "I'll call you Sky. It goes with the height and your purty blue eyes. So tell me, Sky, do you ride?"

"Uh, ride? Oh, you mean horses," he added sheepishly after he remembered where he was. "No, ma'am, not yet. But I hope to learn."

"We'll start this afternoon," Letty announced with

the air of a general commanding troops. "You won't win any prizes by Sunday, but I can promise you'll be able to stay in the saddle." She let out a raucous cackle. "Promise your sitter will be sore, too—"

"Now, Letty," Bentley broke in, "I told you we came here to discuss Lowell's contract. He has to report for rookie camp Sunday afternoon and I don't want him showing up walking funny."

Letty cackled again, then herded them inside her cool native-stone house. As always, Bentley was drawn to the expansive windows designed to take advantage of the scenic vistas surrounding Letty's hilltop home. "I forget how beautiful it is here," she murmured, gazing out at the austere haunting beauty of the hill country.

The attraction to this land defied description, but once experienced, the impact was strong and lasting. Much about it was hard—spare and desolate, even as it yielded up its strange brand of solace. The landscape endured, untamed by time or man, giving comfort to those who succumbed to its mystical appeal.

It reminded her of Reid.

After they were settled and had eaten an early supper, Letty fulfilled her promise to give Sky his first riding lesson. Bentley chuckled as she watched them start out across the pasture at a sedate pace. Sky dwarfed his docile mare while little Letty sat easily astride a prancing gelding. Sky might as well enjoy himself while he could. Beginning tomorrow, he would be tested.

That night before they retired, she cornered him in the den. She didn't want the real reason for their being there to be far from his mind. "First thing in the morning, I'd like to initiate the talks regarding your contract."

Sky bounded off the sofa where he'd been reclining.

Immediately the room diminished in size. "I'm not interested in the business end of things. I'm out of my element with that kind of stuff."

"I understand," Bentley said, her head tipped back so she could see his face. "Perhaps we should get in touch with your agent or lawyer, whomever will represent you." She'd found it extremely odd that the person had failed to contact her already. She hoped they weren't planning to stage a holdout. That would put her on even shakier ground.

"I don't have either."

"You . . . *what*?" The concept was so foreign, so incredible, so impossible, that she might have laughed had she not seen that Sky was dead serious. "You mean you have no one to advise you in the matter of your Titan contract?"

"What's to advise about? I want to play basketball and the team obviously wants me to do it for them. I can't see that there will be any major obstacles to prevent that."

Bentley sprang from her chair and latched on to his arm, subtly steering him back to the couch. When he was seated, she could better look him in the eye. "Lowell, I'm sure you're aware that you are in a position to command a very large salary, plus signing bonus and other compensation."

He shrugged again. Didn't he realize the world was full of unscrupulous people who would pick his innocent bones unless he took steps to prevent it? She could already see long lines of slick operators ready to sell him the merits of their get-rich-quick schemes. He needed protecting.

Theoretically it wasn't her job; ethically, Bentley knew she couldn't stand by and let that happen. She tried again. "You'll be a wealthy young man, Lowell, and although the Titans won't divulge numbers, there will be some fairly accurate speculation about how much you'll be earning."

"There's nothing I can do to prevent people from guessing about that, but I still don't see why we need to rush all this contract business."

Bentley felt like telling him they were hardly rushing it. Had he been like most draftees, he'd have wanted to come to terms ASAP so he could start spending his money.

"Let me give you an idea of what to expect. Before long you'll start hearing from friends whose names you don't recognize. Relatives you don't recall meeting will crawl out of the woodwork. Every one of them will have a sure-fire idea for using your money to make even more."

He looked utterly shocked. She had reached him at last. "For that reason, it's vital to get the legalities taken care of so you and your financial adviser can come up with an investment plan."

He gawked at her, horror etched on his face. "I don't know anything about investments. Don't want to, either."

"All the more reason to hire someone to help you."

"I'll give it some thought."

"If I may make a suggestion," she ventured. "I know an attorney who specializes in financial planning. He's been a friend of my family for years. I trust him completely and will personally vouch for his integrity." Luckily, George Martin had relocated to Austin, a half-hour drive away. "With your permission, I'll give him a call and ask him to meet us here in the morning."

She hoped her luck held and George would be able to rearrange his schedule to accommodate her.

"I guess that would be all right," he finally conceded. When Sky rose, Bentley knew she wasn't going to get any more out of him tonight. In his own way, this giant with the choir-boy face was every bit as mulish and maddening as Reid. And she was caught between the two.

But if it was the last act she performed as a Maverick employee, she would deliver Lowell Hawkins to rookie camp with business taken care of.

Friday brought Bentley renewed faith that there was justice in the world. Either that or divine intervention. George and his secretary arrived early. At noon they were well on their way to reaching an agreement. By evening, they had refined all the points of a multi-page contract. The only thing that remained was typing the final copy and getting it signed by the principals.

She liked to think that all the groundwork she'd been laying over the last agonizing weeks had helped things proceed so smoothly. Or perhaps it had been George's folksy, low-key way of explaining the complicated document that had gained Sky's confidence right away.

At this point she didn't care who or what deserved the credit. She was only glad to get free of the strain she'd been under. Letty fed them a late dinner before George and his secretary headed back to Austin.

Bentley went to bed with happy thoughts zinging around inside her head for the first time in ages. Tomorrow she would call Reid and surprise him with the good news. She hoped it would be adequate compensation for the fact that she had skipped town without leaving word as to where she was going. Only her mother knew she had gone to visit Letty, and even Victoria hadn't been told about Sky.

First thing Saturday morning when Bentley dialed the office, hoping to catch Reid, she got Marian instead. "Be sure to relay the message when you see him," she told his secretary with a mixture of relief and disappointment.

"I wouldn't want to deprive you of that honor." Marian cleared her throat. "Besides, you can tell him yourself."

"I thought you said he isn't there."

"That's right. He's on his way to Kerrville."

"What? He's coming here? But that's impossible." She massaged her forehead. How could learning of Reid's arrival give her a headache so quickly? "How did he find out where we are?"

"He mentioned something about asking Paul Westlake."

Under orders from his boss to come up with Bentley's whereabouts, Paul would naturally call Victoria. Knowing that Bentley and Paul were longtime friends, Victoria wouldn't hesitate to tell him about Bentley's trip to the hill country. "Oh, no," she moaned. "Then he's—"

"Loaded for bear is the expression, I believe."

Bentley moaned again. For the rest of the morning she paced and planned. And waited.

Before she heard the hum of an engine as it climbed the hill, Bentley felt a little shock wave traverse her spine. How she knew Reid was near remained a mystery. She just *knew*. The doorbell rang in confirmation.

As she crossed the stone foyer, she tightened the purple-and-gold twist belt of her teal jumpsuit. Hand

on the knob, she hesitated only long enough to draw
in a single deep breath. Then she swept open the door.

"Mr. Hunter. Won't you come in?" Lord, it was
hard to sound gracious with that regiment of butterflies
at war in her stomach. And, Lord, he looked good after
days of not seeing him. Taller, leaner. Meaner.

Suddenly she didn't care if he was mad as the very
devil at her. She'd gladly put up with his wrath just to
be close to him.

"North." His voice didn't reveal a trace of emotion
. . . at first. "A cozy little hideaway you have here."

He hadn't looked at anything but her so how could
he tell? "I, uh, thought I could manage things with
Sky better if we were out of the spotlight."

"Mmm," he said, still watching her. "Seems more
like a place for fun and . . . relaxation."

Bentley knew Sky had developed a crush on her. Did
Reid suspect? Possibly, if she read the taunt in his
voice correctly. "Why don't we go into the library?
Lowell and I were about to have some tea." She led
him to the comfortably shabby book-lined room, its
spaciousness dwarfed by the two big men.

Unaware of the undercurrents between Reid and
Bentley, and unaccustomed to dealing with the man
who now owned his services, Sky offered his hand in
a friendly greeting.

Bentley held her breath while Reid studied the hand.
At last he took it, the shake as brief as his terse,
"Hawkins." Reid's eyes flicked toward the door, then
back at the young man. "Bentley and I have some
things to settle. I'm sure you can find something to
occupy you. Somewhere else."

Sky might not be familiar with everything that was
going on, but he was perceptive. He looked to Bentley,

who nodded. Before he closed the door, Sky said, "I'll be out by the pool if you need anything."

She smiled at his gallant gesture, but in spite of his height advantage, Lowell Hawkins would never be tough enough to defy Reid Hunter. She wondered if *anyone* would ever be that tough.

"Do you think you'll need a protector, Bentley?"

"You tell me," she said, her throat tight, though not from fear. His voice did the most wicked things to her, and at the most inopportune times. She ought to be concentrating on defending herself instead of. . . .

Adopting his favored stance, he propped himself against the door to an adjoining powder room. "I'd say at best, you deserve a blistering lecture."

"And at worst?"

"I'll leave the worst to your imagination."

Deciding she had nothing to lose, Bentley faced him from behind the library table. "Before you start the lecture, you should know that Sky's contract is a fait accompli." That surprised him, but only momentarily.

"When?"

"We finished late last night."

"You have it?" he asked, making no move when she nodded and tapped a thick stack of paper on the table.

"Terms?"

"Basically, we're talking ten million over six years," she said matter-of-factly, schooling herself not to gloat.

He whistled and transferred his hands to the front pocket of his jeans. "I was prepared to pay more. A lot more."

She allowed herself a brief self-satisfied smile. Because she'd hooked Sky up with George they had signed a separate agreement whereby George worked on a flat-fee annual retainer, instead of taking the exorbitant percentage cut of typical sports agents. The difference saved the Titans big bucks. "Maybe you should forego the tongue-lashing and tell me what a good job I did."

He threw back his head and laughed. "I always knew you were one sharp little bargainer, North. In fact, you just talked yourself out of a lecture." He started toward her. "But the tongue-lashing . . . well, honey, that's something I can't resist."

He stopped a short distance away, resting his hips on the back of an overstuffed sofa. "Come out from behind there, Bentley. Take your punishment like a woman."

"And if I don't?"

What he told her was so explicitly naughty she didn't dare test him. Instead she rounded the table slowly, desiring not dreading his punishment. The pure sensual fire in his eyes held the promise of pleasure, not pain.

He circled her wrist and tugged her between his outstretched legs. "No more business for the rest of the weekend. Just pleasure. Let's start with your mouth, and we'll go on from there."

EIGHT

Bentley pressed herself close, trembling with need. She needed so much from this man. His strength, his vitality made her feel more alive than she did when they were apart.

Anticipating the taste of him, craving the stimulation of his mustache moving over her, she closed her eyes. Her lips parted, the aura of expectation hung heavy.

"Where in Hades is everyone?" Letty burst into the room, her face rosy with exertion. She gave no indication that she'd noticed Bentley's startled leap away from Reid or heard the oath he uttered through gritted teeth. "Well, hello there," she said, studying Reid. "It would seem this is my weekend for gentleman callers."

Reid was a little slow getting to his feet, and Bentley stepped between him and Letty, performing introductions as she moved. He unfolded at last, his large hand swallowing Letty's smaller one. "It would seem I'm indebted to you. I was beginning to wonder if I'd ever see a contract. Then North sneaks off to your place with Hawkins and gets the job done in one day."

"It's the air over here. Makes thinking easier," Letty explained ingenuously. "Anyway, the reason I'm looking for everybody is that lunch is ready."

They gathered in the big country kitchen, and during the course of their meal, Bentley noticed that Reid's earlier irritation with Lowell had seemingly evaporated. No doubt he figured he'd gotten his no-trespassing message across to the younger man.

After lunch Letty declared she was going to take Sky rock-hunting on a remote corner of her property. "Want to go along?" she asked Bentley with a fey smile.

"No thanks. I think I'll just hang out around the pool. Maybe even take a nap." Her glare defied Letty to make a comment, but the woman's attention was already fixed on Reid.

"Guess I don't need to bother asking you to come." The smile rivaled Reid's at its slyest.

He grinned and stretched like an oversize feline. "I'm kind of tired, too."

Bentley couldn't help giggling, but the juvenile reaction exasperated her. Reid was almost never tired and right now he looked quite lively. The pledge in his eyes turned her insides warm and fluid. Maybe lying in the sun wasn't such a good idea. She didn't need to get any hotter. A dip in the pool just might offset the heat Reid always generated in her. She excused herself and went to put on a bathing suit.

Within minutes, she stood at pool's edge, waving to Letty and Sky as they trotted away. She and Reid were alone for the first time since she'd come to terms with loving him. Her nerve endings tingled with barely suppressed excitement. Her pulse echoed with the rhythm that signaled, today, today. She stood straight, poised to dive.

Bentley didn't see, didn't hear, until it was too late. Momentum catapulted them both into the pool. She heard herself scream just before she hit the water, a ragged, horror-stricken wail of anguish.

The disembodied voice had followed her here, had caught up with her at last, was going to finish her off in defiance of Reid's best efforts.

Reid knew something was wrong, very wrong, the instant his body collided with Bentley's and propelled them into the water. Her cry was not from surprise, nor was it a token protest against what he had intended as playful rowdiness. Her shriek had been piercing, chilling, born of terror.

He reacted before they broke the water's surface, wrapping his arms around her. Twisting so he would land on his back, he absorbed the greatest impact of their plunge. But it wasn't easy.

Her arms and legs thrashed wildly, fighting him, fighting the water, as her head went under, bobbed up, then disappeared again in the churning foam. In the seconds before he could rescue her, she struggled even more. Reid touched bottom, shot back to the surface, and grabbed Bentley with one arm, clamping her against his chest. With his other arm, he took quick, powerful strokes to the shallow end of the pool.

As soon as he could stand and lift her out of the water, he began walking toward the steps. Still she fought, as if her survival depended on continual motion. Reid's muscles strained against her resistance until he laid her on a wide chaise lounge. He stretched out and got both arms around her, using one leg to pin her ankles.

Despite the warm water and baking sun, she felt icy cold and she shook uncontrollably. "Idiot," he muttered under his breath, cursing himself for seven kinds of fool. He smoothed Bentley's soaked hair away from her face.

"Honey, it's all right. *You're* all right." He tried to make his voice sound soothing, but his own delayed reaction had him feeling shaky, too. Why hadn't he been smart enough to know Bentley hadn't completely shed the fear and edginess she'd been living under for months?

"I'm sorry, sweetheart. I didn't mean to scare you, and you know I'd never hurt you. I swear."

Her eyes were wide, unfocused and dilated with fright. She didn't seem to be aware of who he was. The shivering increased and he blanketed her body fully with his. With one hand he kneaded the back of her neck. The other he used to massage her arm, trying to restore warmth.

"Bentley, it's okay," he repeated. She blinked and he saw reality return. He kissed her then, letting his heat flow between them, using his mouth as slowly and as deftly as he could manage.

When she began to respond, he whispered in her ear—meaningless words, calming words that suddenly transformed into words of passion. He felt her stir beneath his heavy weight and she looked deeply into his eyes.

"I can't believe I did this again. Why do I always turn into a hopelessly hysterical simpleton when you're around to witness it?"

He drew away a fraction, supporting himself on one elbow. "Stop blaming yourself. I have seen you really upset two times, one of which my carelessness caused."

"No, I overreacted, plain and simple." Her gaze

lowered before she forced it back up to meet his. "It's just that for those few seconds . . ."

"I know. You thought *he'd* come to get you. Too bad that didn't occur to me until too late. I ought to have known you're still dealing with some residual hangups from that ordeal. Will you let me get by with pleading stupidity?"

She shook her head. "No, I will not. As you said, it's my hangup and I have to learn to deal with it better. Most of the time it is better, since we got back from New York." Her teeth worked at her bottom lip, as if the admission had cost her some pride. "Today it was just the surprise. I wasn't expecting . . . Look, can't we forget this happened at all?"

He could see her struggle. She made such an issue of being strong and independent, as if she had to prove something to him. "Sure. I'm willing if you are."

"I'm . . . willing." He watched her watch a drop of water snake down his chest. When she blotted it with her index finger, then touched her tongue, he thought he'd lose it all right there. "Oh, Reid, kiss me."

Fighting to keep a tight rein, he let his lips graze her temple, dip briefly to her mouth, wander lower to rest against her neck. His hand resumed its-lazy stroking of her inner arm. If he could just remember to take it slow. He didn't want to do anything to startle or frighten her again.

"Is that all you want?" she asked breathlessly.

"No." His breathing quickened. Audibly.

"The Reid Hunter I know would take what he wants."

Yep, he was going to lose it for sure. His mouth covered hers, lingered for as long as he could without moving, until desire overcame control and he pulled back. His tongue stole out, but he wet his own lips.

"Bentley, don't disappear again without telling me. I always want to know where you are. I need to."

"I was only doing my job. My boss demands so much."

"Your boss is about to get very demanding."

At last, Bentley mused, just before he groaned and fused their mouths with a kiss so arousing that there was no mistaking the nature of his demands. She had never experienced evocative images like Reid inspired with his tongue. It licked with rhythmic insistence at the juncture of her lips, and when she opened them in invitation, it surged inside like the bold marauder he was.

But once inside, he seemed to regard her mouth as treasure to be savored, not subdued. His tongue gentled, setting a languorous pace for their pleasure. It traced an indolent circle around the softness of her inner lips, delved beneath hers to find an even softer haven, stroked the ridges behind her teeth.

Bentley's tongue met his, matched his moves in a slow, sinuous mating dance made all the more seductive by its lack of urgency. She needed no further prompting when Reid lifted her arms slightly so he could fit his hands around the curve of her waist. Her hands glided up his arms to rest on his shoulders; her thumbs dipped into the furrows behind his collarbones, lightly rubbing the taut skin.

He gave her ear the same avid attention he'd devoted to her mouth and Bentley felt herself dissolving, melting into Reid as if her bones had liquefied. Her arms draped over his, too weak to cling.

She gasped as his lips moved, and a new wave of

sensation washed over her. She'd never known that the insides of her elbows were so deliciously responsive to erotic exploration. Reid sucked at the delicate skin there, like a hungry man devouring luscious fruit.

"Oh!" Her word was impelled out on a soft swell of air. He had lifted her to a higher plateau, nibbling at the indentation of her waist, then easing the tiny stings with tongue baths. The sparks and flashes and explosions within her were as brilliant as fireworks.

Just when she was in danger of swooning, he sat up and looked at her. She felt as though an essential part of her had been yanked away, leaving her incomplete. Eyes lambent, she silently implored him not to stop.

"Bentley, I'm not a patient man. I've waited as long as I can to see all of you." His gaze dropped to her breasts, measured their rise and fall beneath the inadequate shield of two microscopic black patches. His eyes turned dark with arousal. She could feel what he was seeing.

Her breath backed up in her throat. How could her mouth feel so dry when the rest of her was flowing like a river in spring?

Their eyes met again, and after a prolonged moment of unspoken request and consent, Reid brought one hand to the bow behind her neck. Gazes still locked, he slowly pulled the string until it extended full length. Then he released it so both straps fell to her sides.

Because she was half reclining, Bentley felt the triangles slip down, but she froze a breath away from being fully exposed to Reid. She couldn't breathe.

"Untie the other one for me."

Giving herself up to the raspy lure of his voice and the overt eroticism of what he'd told her to do, she closed her eyes. When she opened them again, Bentley looked at him confidently, proudly, and with a single motion of her wrist, loosened and discarded the bikini top.

"God!"

His assessment was so fiery, so intense, that for a second she wondered if her skin would burst into flame before her heart pounded her to death from the inside.

"I have fantasized for weeks about how you're going to taste." He opened his mouth in prelude and bent his head. She watched his tongue touch her for an instant before his lips closed over the breast she had bared so brazenly, offered so wantonly.

His mouth was hot and wet and ravenous, taking her, drawing her in, paying homage with his tongue. "Sweet," he said hoarsely, and tasted some more.

Bentley moaned a nearly soundless plea when he released her. But the respite was brief, only for the time it took him to capture her other nipple and lavish it with equal adulation. She cried out at the deep, aching sensation, a primal affirmation of her femininity that she felt in every part of her.

He had no right to be this accomplished, she thought, damning him for all the women he must have known to get that way. And then she blessed him when his hand found her in a caress so intimate, it sent an electrifying surge all the way to her toes.

Slumberously, she watched him work his way down her body. His mustache, dark and sable soft, painted exquisite brushstrokes over her breasts and down her stomach, halting just before he reached the remaining barrier.

Bentley arched into him, malleable as pure gold in the hands of a skilled artisan, bending to become the creation he shapes.

"Reid, I—"

"Yes, honey. Tell me what you need." His fingers slipped inside the elastic of her bikini, spreading to shape her.

"Oh, please . . ."

Reid swore mightily. His hands stilled.

Bentley heard the intrusive whap-whap of helicopter blades overhead and wanted to scream. Damn Letty's globetrotting neighbor for spoiling the mood.

"I want you like hell, Bentley. But something tells me this is not the time or place for the kind of thing I have in mind." He reached for a towel to cover her. "Why don't you scoot inside and put on something ugly and baggy before I forget my good intentions?"

She wrapped the terry cloth around her, feeling frustrated and irritable because, as usual, Reid was calling the shots. He was much too adept at turning on and turning off. Wasn't sex the one thing women were supposed to control?

She stood and began to walk away, her steps stiff and faltering.

"Bentley, there's one thing before you go. I need to hear you say that you trust me to make sure nobody will hurt you. Can you give me that?"

She didn't turn around, preferring to analyze her options without having to confront the full force of Reid. Withholding the trust he seemed to need might be a way of establishing some power for herself. But she would be cheating them both by being less than honest. The truth was she did believe Reid capable of overcoming any hurdle, including a crime boss's threats.

"I trust you to do exactly what you've said you will," she said in a husky voice. Verbalizing it reinforced her conviction. "I no longer fear for my life."

"I knew I could convince you."

She refused to turn and face the satisfaction she heard in his voice. Instead she hurried to her room, locked the door, and took to her bed like a Victorian maiden with vapors. The stress of negotiating Sky's contract, Reid's unexpected arrival, the catastrophe in the pool, and her subsequent acquiescence to his demand of trust had put her through an emotional wringer.

She slept for nearly four hours, and by the time she'd showered and dressed in a red cotton skirt and patterned sweater, Letty and Sky had taken off for Kerrville to eat dinner out. Reid, however, was still there.

"Are you all right now?" he asked.

"I'm fine. Just needed to do a little catch-up sleeping."

"Good. Let's hit the road."

"Are we meeting Letty and Sky?"

"No. It's just the two of us."

"Good," she said, quivering when a sound rolled out of him, deep and stirring and probably dangerous.

He led her to a car parked in the circular front drive. She'd never seen it before, but recognized right away that it had to belong to Reid. The black Porsche looked just like its owner—dark, self-contained, and lethal.

"A status symbol, Mr. Hunter? I'm surprised."

"I don't care anything for symbols. I do what I want, buy what I want, for me, not to impress."

That summed up the way he did everything, she thought. Charging through life in a straight line, aiming for the goal and bulldozing obstructions out of his path.

Even before he slammed her door, Bentley sensed she was in for some ride. Watching Reid stride lithely around the car like some great stalking cat only confirmed it. He claimed the driver's seat and said, "Buckle up, North. This sucker moves."

She fumbled for her seat belt and clicked it into place while he revved the engine. Then they rocketed down the drive like a cannon shot. He decelerated only briefly when the mile-long ranch road met paved highway and he downshifted into the turn.

Strapped so close to him Bentley was keenly aware of how completely he dominated the confined space. Both hands on the wheel, he drove with a relentless absorption that attracted her almost as much as it repelled her. More evidence of his energy and control.

"Come on, you hot little number, show me your stuff."

She opened her mouth to complain, then realized he was speaking to the car, as if his whole world consisted of man and Porsche. Bentley felt herself slipping into the same rhythm, swaying and vibrating in time with the vehicle.

He shifted and banked into a curve at an alarming rate of speed, shifted again for the straightaway. "Come on, baby, talk to me."

The mighty engine responded, and so did she. Her skin heated, throbbed as if it had been stroked by searing hands. She squirmed restlessly in the leather cocoon of her seat. They streaked through the darkness, connected by the polarity that linked them, a magic so potent it seemed to have a life force of its own.

"Reid, please," she moaned, though she wasn't begging for his restraint. "Slow down."

"Not yet. Not yet!"

Bentley eyed the speedometer. So fast. Much too fast. But her imagination was racing at an even faster pace. Reid's symbolic seduction was having such a profound effect she couldn't sit still.

"Don't let up now. Just a little more. I want to hear you scream!"

The scream reverberated inside Bentley's head as the car obeyed. Their speed climbed, peaked, held until she knew the scream would escape. Then, Reid lifted his foot from the pedal and slowed them to a coast.

He grasped the wheel, shuddering. "Ah, yes. You are one fine piece of work."

Bentley sagged against her seat belt, totally wrung out. In the green iridescence of the instrument panel, she examined his face. He looked equally spent.

His eyes cut to her. "Tell me what you want to do now."

Bentley was certain her heart could not survive any more punishment that day. "You'd better take me back."

Neither spoke during the return trip. When he stopped, he didn't kill the engine. "Get in the house, Bentley. I am hot and hungry and hard. If you're half as smart as we both know you are, you'll put a locked door between us. And fast."

NINE

Sunday afternoon Bentley dropped off Sky at the Houston campus where the Titan's rookie camp was being held. His last-minute appearance was the lead story on all the local news programs, eclipsing even a major Oiler victory.

When reporters descended en masse, she felt an almost maternal protective urge. From now on, Sky's every move would be open to media scrutiny. But he was in the big time now and had to fend for himself. Before leaving him, though, she made sure he would call her if he ever needed help with anything.

The next morning she met with Jim Lawson. For the first time since she'd joined Maverick, the head of the legal department—not Reid—would be directing her activities.

She'd gotten used to working closely with Reid. On the other hand, when she didn't have to see him at the office, didn't have to report to him, it would be almost as though she didn't work for him. That would make it so much easier for them to explore their personal relationship.

There was no point in delaying what Reid had weeks ago pronounced inevitable. Saturday he had awakened a passion so consuming that it frightened her. All those incipient longings must have been slumbering inside her, undisturbed and waiting, waiting for him to bring them to life.

Certain she'd hear from him after arriving home Sunday, Bentley had maintained a vigil beside her silent phone until past midnight. The irony of willing her phone to ring didn't escape her. All day Monday she had to keep reminding herself that she was a professional. Otherwise she'd have called him. It distressed her to realize she might be turning into that kind of woman.

His call finally came that night. He'd been tied up all day in Washington, D.C., but his voice conveyed barely suppressed enthusiasm. He was one of a small delegation of American business executives invited to travel to several Russian states to work out an exchange of technology. Despite his predictions that the personal computer market was softening, he could not turn down a coup like selling his product in the newly emerging Russian economy.

The hitch was, he had to leave right away. Bentley tried to share his enthusiasm, but she could only see his good fortune in terms of the personal cost to her. Just when she had begun to feel positive about a future with Reid, they were going to be separated.

He told her he'd be gone only a couple of weeks and that he was sorry as hell. She was sorry, too.

Pulsing with impatience, Reid paced while he waited interminably for the call to go through. These foreign telephone systems sucked. The hotel food wasn't all that thrilling, either, though he'd been assured it had improved greatly in the past year.

He was just out of sorts in general because he missed Bentley. How he wished he were with her, and that he didn't have to make this call. Especially at this time, when he knew her phone would be ringing in the middle of the night. He cursed and paced some more, hoping she might somehow sense it was him and not be terrified to pick up.

When the connection was finally made and she answered, he swallowed. Twice. "Bentley, God, I miss you."

"Reid! Oh, Reid, please say you're in Houston," she said, though she could undoubtedly tell that he wasn't. "I'll die if you say you have to stay there longer." His two weeks had already expanded to four.

"No, I'll be leaving Moscow tomorrow."

"So you'll be home day after at the latest?"

His free hand formed a fist. He wanted to smash something, anything, with it. "Not exactly."

"You're making a stopover? Where?"

"China," he stated bluntly. He heard her sigh. His stomach didn't feel very steady. "I don't want to, but I have to."

"I've told myself to expect this," she said in a calm, detached voice. "I know you're a busy man with lots of demands on you, priorities you must see to. It's just that I've suddenly discovered I'm selfish."

Reid absorbed another sigh and his fist connected with a wall. "I've been trying to negotiate construction of a soft-drink bottling plant in China for the past few years. But with the Chinese, you wait until they invite you."

"They invited?" She sounded tired. And resigned.

"I just got word yesterday. They want to talk, and now that they're ready, well, it makes sense to go. It'll be simpler if I fly east from here."

"I understand."

"Do you really? All I want to do is be with you, and everything is conspiring against me. I think about you all the time." To compound his misery, his body reacted to those thoughts with alarming frequency.

"In the four weeks since I last saw you, I've had plenty of time to think about us. I know I'll always have to wait my turn, be second or third choice for you." There was a long pause. "I've decided I'll settle for that. Because I think you're worth what little time I can have."

He grimaced and rubbed his eyes. "Bentley, this is killing me. I don't want you to settle for second best. I want to give you everything." He had the need to share with her in a way he'd never done with anyone before.

"I don't expect promises, Reid. Spare us both and don't make them. Just come back as soon as you can. I'll be waiting."

He didn't like the sound of this. The Bentley he knew would never be so long-suffering. His Bentley was used to getting what she wanted. She wouldn't be content with any man's sometime love. He felt oddly panicked and desperate.

Reid had always been able to think quickly. There were instances where that ability had been his salvation. He could feel Bentley slipping away from him, no matter what she said. He had to come up with a way to tie her to him while he was away, something personal, apart from her job. He seized upon the first thing that occurred to him.

"I need you to take care of something for me while I'm gone. Will you do that?" If she consented, he'd have a slim assurance that she'd at least be thinking of him.

"If I can. What is it?"

"I want you to fix up my beach house in Rockport. Do whatever you like, and do it exactly as you would if you were decorating it for yourself. I'll get in touch with Marian and arrange for an account to cover the bills. You can get the key from her tomorrow."

"Reid, are you sure?"

"I'm sure. And Bentley . . . ?"

"Yes?"

"We'll go there and spend some time alone when I get back."

"I'll do my best to make it nice for you."

She hung up then, leaving him with the feeling that they'd taken care of some business. And she hadn't said what he really wanted to hear. That she loved him and missed him.

For the first time he could ever recall, Reid downed a double cognac. It kept him awake for forty-eight straight hours.

It would take three, possibly four, weeks to handle the business in China. Bentley remembered that Reid had said that very specifically. She wanted to believe him.

Communication from the People's Republic was slow, sporadic, and unreliable. They tried to have several phone conversations, but those turned out to be disappointing and unsatisfying.

It was a good thing her job had become more and more demanding. She needed to push herself, to keep from thinking about what she wanted and couldn't have.

She loved the beach house at first glance. Armed only with a sleeping bag, notebook, and tape measure, Bentley spent her first weekend in Rockport planning. She returned to Houston full of visions. The following Saturday she met with a local contractor and gave him instructions for the first phase of the redo, along with the promise of a bonus if the work was completed ahead of schedule.

The next time she went down, a crew had laid white ceramic tiles throughout the octagonal-shaped house. Pale-aqua grasscloth wallpaper would go up the next week, then she could add the finishing touches.

More than once Bentley blessed Reid for suggesting she do this. It kept her occupied, and it made her feel closer to him. As it turned out, she needed that more than she'd guessed.

The month Reid had expected to spend in China turned into another week, then on and on until she'd lost track of how long he'd been away. The few times they talked, his frustration hummed through the wires. And she was as fidgety and irritable as Reid at his worst.

When it appeared that he wouldn't even get back for the first Titans exhibition game, Bentley was more depressed and disappointed than she'd ever been in her life. Fate was scheming against them and she began to believe she'd never see Reid again.

For much the same reason she'd so readily agreed to decorate his beach house, she flew to Milwaukee for the game. His basketball team was high on Reid's list of priorities right now. Following their progress was a means of staying close to him in spirit.

The game was full of fast-paced action and the lead seesawed often. Sky delivered an impressive debut performance and the Titans won. The victory would have been so much sweeter if she'd been able to share it with Reid.

To make matters worse, after she decided to walk back to the Athletic Club, where Marian had made her reservations, a storm front moved through the city, plummeting temperatures and filling the skies with thick, wet snow. Naturally, there wasn't a taxi in sight.

She'd just toweled off after a hot shower and slipped on a champagne-colored satin robe when an authoritative knock shook the door.

She froze, but almost immediately relaxed. She didn't have to wonder who it was; a very primal female instinct told her. Exhilaration coursed through her and she made no effort to contain it. She'd wanted this too long for moderation to be an option. She threw open the door, not caring how overanxious she appeared.

"Cold enough for you?"

"Reid!" His hair was longer than usual, his voice rougher. The lines etching his face betrayed the exhaustion he must be feeling. Bentley embraced him in a burst of pent-up yearning. Her hands and lips flowed over him, boldly asserting her intention to make up for the weeks they'd been apart, and not to waste any time getting started.

When at last she drew away to gaze up at him, he stepped inside the room and locked the door, never taking his eyes off her. Bentley had never seen a man who looked and tasted and felt so wonderful. How could she have been so chilled a short time ago, when with one question, he'd warmed her to the flash point?

"I'd say it's getting hotter and hotter." She threw

herself against him again. Her eager hands pushed aside his navy overcoat, snaked their way around his cashmere-sweatered chest, pulled the shirt from his waistband. She sighed when she made contact with the warm, sleek skin of his back.

It was as if she'd spent a lifetime anticipating this one moment, an instant so sublime it filled her with awe. She couldn't stop touching him, it didn't matter where. She had to reassure herself he was real, that he wouldn't vanish. Too many of her nighttime visions had faded to fantasies which eluded her when she reached out for them. Her fingers skimmed over his face, outlined his ears, trailed down his chest. And her mouth followed greedily.

"Lord, honey. Go easy on me, will you? Five months is one hell of a long time to want you." He stilled her hands. "I'm trying to hold on, but my self-control is almost non-existent."

She jumped back, searching his face. "You mean that since—"

"Yes."

"And you haven't—"

"No."

She had hoped, but didn't dare believe, that Reid would have waited all this time for her. He was her dream come true, her fantasy personified. And he'd just told her she meant enough to him that he wouldn't settle for a substitute. She could hardly contain her joy.

Bentley smiled, her eyes aglow with promise. She'd show him she was worth the wait. "I know patience doesn't come naturally."

"Give me credit for trying. For a change, I wanted to do something right with you." He buried one hand in her hair, then just as quickly withdrew it and walked over to the window.

"Reid?"

Staring out into the night, he kneaded the back of his neck. "I don't know how it happened, but all of a sudden I feel about sixteen years old. My hands are sweating, my mouth's dry, and my heartbeat is about to choke me." He finally turned to face her. "How can being with you do all that?"

Bentley spoke with the certainty of shared feelings. "Because you do the same to me. Because it took so long to find each other. Because it's important." She glided across the room to touch him on the shoulder. "Let's not wait any longer."

"The first day I saw you, I wanted you."

"I knew that. But I had to ignore it. Then." Now she was shaking with anticipation.

"You can't ignore it now."

"I don't want to."

Still, he hesitated. Then he shrugged out of his coat and peeled the red sweater over his head, tossing both onto a corner chair. Bentley stood immobile, mentally discarding his dark flannel slacks and tattersall shirt as he came toward her.

"It's been eighty-four days since I've kissed you. Don't expect me to get enough anytime soon."

She loved the gritty resonance of his voice in her ear, loved that he'd counted the time, as she had. She wanted to tell him all that, but his mouth fastened on hers, and after that, words were as unnecessary as they were impossible. She couldn't think of anything beyond the magnitude of her feelings for Reid, and how perfectly right it was for them to be together, at last.

Months of repressed longing broke loose, as if interior gates could no longer withstand the combined forces of their passion. He framed the back of her neck with one hand, his other arm pulled her to him so tightly she felt the heat and texture of him branding her breasts through the gossamer-thin satin.

Her breath escaped on a sigh as her head tipped back against his hand, and she willingly tendered all she had to give. His lips roamed restlessly across her cheek, along the angle of her jaw, down her neck, as though the heated flesh could appease his hunger.

He pressed his mouth against the visible pulse at the base of her throat, and his satisfied growl told her he had measured the depth of her need as surely as if she'd told him with words. His tongue and mustache moved in tandem, first sampling, then devouring, setting off an explosive pounding through her veins.

A series of small involuntary tremors rocked Bentley and she pulled back, shivering from a surfeit of pleasure. But Reid's hold tightened, arching her back over his arm, forcing her hips against his steely length and offering her breasts as tribute to his impatient mouth.

Her nipples contracted under the implied caress of his gaze, and the robe was meager protection when he bent his head and dampened the satin, then tugged at the sensitive tip, his teeth gentle but insistent.

"Please," Bentley whispered, and her hands showed him how. Her fingers plunged into the thickness of his hair, guiding as he pushed aside the robe, holding when his mouth closed over her, pressing when the measured suction of his lips and tongue wasn't enough. "Oh, Reid . . ."

He tore his mouth away, his breath unsteady. "We'd better get closer to the bed before it's too late."

Her laugh was a shaky expulsion of tension, because

his control seemed as tenuous as hers. Which reassured her. She didn't want him to have this kind of mastery over her unless he was equally vulnerable.

She urged his mouth to join hers, and with every darting invasion of her tongue, Bentley edged back a step, drawing him with her until they reached the bed. In one graceful move, she sank to the mattress, bringing Reid along with her.

The lure of his already aroused body bearing down on hers was so flagrantly sensual that she gasped and lifted herself against him. The feel of them fitting together, like erotic puzzle pieces, elevated her to a plane where nothing existed apart from the two of them.

Bentley's long-ago impressions rushed back to envelop her. Reid was solid, powerful, unyielding, demanding, possessive . . . and overwhelmingly desirable.

His lips were questing, grazing her temples, her eyelids, her neck, settling at last over her mouth. He swallowed her moan of satisfaction and lazily rubbed her tongue with his until she moaned again, asking for more.

He sat up and untied the sash of her robe, opening its folds to reveal her completely for the first time. Just before his eyes closed, Bentley saw that they were dark, glittering pools of desire. And then she was sinking. . . .

"Do you have any idea how you look to me right now?" His head dropped back, his face contorted. "Beautiful."

Her lashes fluttered down and she trembled, aflame with the same desire she saw in his eyes. She tried to swallow, but couldn't—spoke, but her voice sounded like a stranger's. "I know I've always looked like this, and that it didn't matter." But when she met his gaze again, she knew it *did* matter. For Reid, she wanted to be beautiful and brilliant and everything else he'd ever want or need.

His eyes traveled over her, all of her, for a very long time. "I thought you looked tempting that first day in my office. And I've lost track of how often I've seen you like this . . . in my mind."

Bentley was having trouble forming words, thoughts. She hadn't expected Reid to seduce her with words. She'd expected him to take her by storm, the way he did everything else. It was the bold, brash Reid she'd fallen in love with, not this too cautious, too deliberate charmer.

His hands slipped inside the robe, resting on her shoulders. "Reality is much better than my imagination."

"I've had some interesting fantasies myself." Her voice sounded whispery, rustling like the satin he was sliding down her arms to free her of the robe.

"You can tell me them. Later." He leaned over her, his fingers shaping the sides of her breasts while his thumbs rested beneath them. Gently he flexed his hands, pressing and lifting her soft flesh up to fill his mouth.

His tongue left hot, slick tracings as it glided from one pebbled crest to the other, circling, coaxing, capturing.

Bentley was delirious with need for him. Her hands latched on to his shirt buttons, then the waist of his slacks. In a frenzy born of deprivation, she touched him everywhere. It wasn't enough. "If I can't see all of you—right now—I'll scream." She didn't exaggerate.

"Take whatever you want, Bentley. Anything you need."

She shook her head, not believing she'd ever wanted

or needed anything this much. She couldn't control her breathing. It rushed out in shallow puffs, making her light-headed.

"You want me, don't you? I can hear it." He bit her ear. Hard. "I want to hear it all night."

Bentley felt a thin sheen of moisture turn her skin dewy with desire. Reid felt it, too, and ran his tongue over her until she quivered. He was a devilish tormentor, the sting of his teeth igniting her like spark to tinder.

"Please," she begged, but the word had no form, no sound.

"Yes," he answered, the verbalization of her need unnecessary. His hands began a slow, steady descent, and when he found the heart of that need, she welcomed him with a sigh of acceptance and demand. "I can feel it."

There was no mercy in his dexterous, resourceful fingers. He was aggressive, and she acquiesced. When he claimed, she ceded. And always, there was that relentless, gravelly voice vibrating in her ear. Leading, praising, compelling.

But just when he was about to push her into a blissful, solitary oblivion, Bentley held back. "No . . . I want us together, Reid. Together."

Poised on the brink, she watched him stand and strip off his clothes, dropping them with careless haste. Looking down at her, he was gloriously male, wanting her. She drew him back to her, touched him. Satin smooth and diamond hard. So magnificent she wanted to cry. "Oh, Reid. I want you."

"How much?"

"Desperately!"

"Where?"

"Inside me. Deep! Deep!"

"Sweet heaven!" He thrust fiercely, then stiffened, the tautness of his muscles mirrored on his face. "I meant to take more time, make it last longer. Wanted to give you every kind of pleasure you'd ever imagined."

"Having you here is almost more pleasure than I can bear. I wasn't kidding when I said desperate." She ran her forefinger down the center of him, from his throat to where they were locked together. "And I want you as out of control as I am. I want you on fire."

He made a savage sound as his passion gathered force and he became a storm raging all around her. Untamed, he took her quickly to the edge of madness.

They joined, merging and moving as one. The rhythm was recurring, age-old, but for Bentley it was too strong, too essential not to have been created just for them.

Her senses were filled with Reid. *She* was filled with him. Mind, body, soul. He demanded it all.

She clutched at him, opened herself more fully, seeking a closeness that seemed impossible because already not even air separated them.

He pushed her faster. Harder. Higher.

The ecstasy she was straining toward vibrated within her, sending out shock waves, heating her blood, chasing away reason. The need he had sparked threatened to blaze out of control and consume her. But she would not burn alone. "Reid?"

"I'm with you."

She became one with the maelstrom, soaring to a crescendo, sobbing her release in a wild, sweet agony of completion.

And he was with her.

* * *

Reid knew the legal term for what had happened to him. Temporary insanity. He'd had it all worked out in his head. He would take her out to a fine restaurant, buy her the best champagne on the menu, be more charming than he knew how. Then . . . then he'd tell her he loved her. After that, he'd have shown her how much with slow, practiced lovemaking.

So what had he done instead? Gone crazy. Raced through it like an animal. He flopped onto his back and snorted in disgust. "Damn it all!"

Bentley lifted her head, smiled dreamily, and leaned over to kiss his chest. "Calm down, Reid. Making love is supposed to relax you."

"Mmm," he said, mellowing temporarily to return her kiss. "It did more than relax me. It possessed me."

"So what's the problem?" She propped herself up on an elbow and looked at him, eyes bright with interest.

Reid's fingers plowed into his thick, tangled hair. "Dammit, this fouled up all my plans." He grabbed a handful of the rumpled sheet. "Eighty-four days of planning shot to hell in fifteen minutes."

"If that was your fifteen minutes of fame, I'm glad to have participated in it." She gave him a wicked leer. "*Fantastic.*"

Reid sucked in a breath, still weak. Remembering. "God, yes. It was incredible. But it wasn't supposed to be like this." He struggled to sit up, debating whether to tell her about his original plan or to save it for the next night and follow through as intended.

A familiar feeling hit him and he collapsed backward, pounding the bed with one fist. "Aw, hell. Why now? Nothing's going right."

"What's wrong?"

"Honey, I've spent the last twenty-two hours trying

to get here. I've been on boats and trains, airplanes, cabs, even a helicopter. I'm sorry, but I've got to sleep.''

"For two hours?'' she asked, and he recalled the first time he'd been in her bed.

"Yeah, two.'' Turning on his side, he tucked her against him and threw one leg over hers, needing to be sure that she wouldn't leave.

Reid felt himself dropping off, but he whispered one last word. "Mine.''

TEN

Reid willed himself to lie still, to not disturb Bentley. Two hours had passed and, as usual, he was wide awake, all signs of relaxation having fled. He lay tense with the urgency to wake her, but in recent months he'd learned to live with this particular problem. Having her here beside him was enough. He could be content just holding her, watching her sleep.

He'd known ever since New York that he loved Bentley. He'd wanted her even longer than that. But after what they had just shared, he realized he was capable of feelings for which he had no labels.

A strange, powerful emotion swelled inside him, filling him, blocking his throat. He swallowed, and gathered her closer. She was his now, and nothing was ever going to separate them again.

Bentley's eyes opened slowly. She wore a soft, sleepy smile that looked very inviting. He dipped his head to drop a light kiss on her upturned lips. "I didn't mean to wake you. Go back to sleep."

"Not likely with you looking at me like that." Her

stretch was exaggerated and extended, nudging her body against every taut inch of him. "Hmm, you do recharge quickly."

"Two hours? Hardly a record." He rolled onto his back to escape her teasing. It was either that or crush her back into the bedclothes and start all over.

She allowed him to retreat temporarily, taking advantage of the chance to explore the dark terrain of his chest. "Careful, honey," he warned as her fingertips skimmed across his ribs and ventured lower. "You're treading on dangerous ground."

"I know." Her tongue stole out to dampen a nipple. He groaned like a man on a rack, but she continued the punishment, inflaming his senses beyond reason. The faint hint of her perfume mingled with scent of them and he knew a fierce surge of possessiveness.

"Bent-ley." Reid heard his voice, heavy and strained. "Are you sure you want what you're asking for?"

"Am I being too subtle?" Her fingers encircled him, answering the question with one touch.

"My God! Come here!" Shuddering, he pulled her upward, and when she settled atop him, he was inside her. The idea that she would initiate, excited him. The possibility that she'd cause him to lose control as he had two hours ago unnerved him. His hands gripped her waist, he looked into her eyes. "I like you on top, but this time . . ." He began to move, slowly, giving then withholding. Again. Again.

Nothing had ever satisfied him so thoroughly as watching Bentley lose control and let herself be swept away in a rush of pleasure. And when she cried out and melted against him, he brought her down with soothing strokes and approving words. Then he started all over.

"Are you insatiable?"

"I . . . am . . . with . . . you," he got out between flicks of his tongue around her nipples. "I'm . . . not . . . usually."

"I'm not sure I believe that." She laughed shakily and arched to give him greater access. "You do this too well."

"Only because I have the right stimulus. You." His mouth moved up to cover hers, his tongue sliding slowly in and out to parody the languid rhythm of his fingers.

"Oh, Lord, Reid," she gasped and tried to twist away from him. "I don't think I can take any more."

"Try," he urged, his fingers becoming more daring, commanding her response. "Take just a little bit more, and let me feel it."

Reid couldn't tear his eyes away from her. He'd never seen anything more beautiful than Bentley at the moment of her surrender. It was as if a golden aura surrounded her, its shimmering promise reaching out to ensnare him, too. Powerless to resist the ancient lure, he let himself go, chanting her name as he followed her into the dark sanctuary of release.

When they neared Lake Michigan, Bentley tied her red Titans poncho more tightly around her neck. Last night's cold and snow had disappeared along with the storm front which brought them. Only a chilly wind gusting off the lake remained. October snow was one of Mother Nature's freakish tricks, one she'd quickly atoned for with warmer temperatures and clear skies.

Bentley angled her face up to catch the sun's heat, and she had an almost irresistible urge to shout her good fortune to everyone they met. With Reid's arm draped around her shoulders, his warm, strong presence beside her, she felt like the luckiest woman in the world. Being in love with Reid was wonderful. *Making* love with him was sublime. Before long she knew she'd tell him exactly how she felt about him, regardless of the risk.

They'd finally made it down for a late lunch at the Club, after breakfast had been sacrificed to more compelling priorities. In contrast to her earlier repletion, she now felt charged with energy, bursting with the need to be outdoors. As if only the lake's churning surface could provide a dynamic enough counterpoint for her expansive feelings.

When they reached a path which would lead them down an incline to the beach, Reid turned her around to face him. Wordlessly, he spoke to her with his eyes, and then his mouth descended to claim hers. The kiss was neither passionate nor gentle, but rather an affirmation of all they had shared and a commitment to more.

At lake level the wind lashed even more violently, whipping their clothes like tight-masted sails running before a gale. Raising their voices in order to talk seemed like a clamorous intrusion, so they walked for a distance in comfortable silence. In unspoken accord, they climbed another path and chose a park bench overlooking the water.

Reid put his arm around her and Bentley rested her head on his shoulder, staring out at the whitecaps. After a long, quiet interval, she was struck by the improbability of this scene. She had seen him in many situations, many moods, but this was something she never expected to witness. Reid Hunter was relaxed. Totally.

She had noticed that even when he sat completely

still, he gave the impression of being in motion. There was so much going on inside the man that it couldn't be contained. Right now there were no signs of the tumult which usually surrounded him. She drew back slightly and searched his face for clues.

"What?" he asked, toying with the fastening on her poncho.

"I'm just trying to figure out why you're so calm. Normally you'd have been on the phone a couple of dozen times while you got ready to fly off into the wild blue yonder. If I didn't know better, I'd suspect you're taking the day off."

"Saving my energy," he said with a sly grin. "I have plans to expend a lot of it later."

Bentley tried to sound cross, but undermined the attempt by smiling. "What am I going to do with you?"

He whispered in her ear, then laughed when his short, graphic suggestion pinkened her cheeks. "I don't believe my eyes. The always-cool Ms. North blushing."

"Must be this autumn wind," she fibbed smoothly. "It's probably chapping my skin."

"A logical answer for everything." He ruffled her tousled hair. "That's what I like about you." When Bentley gave him a sidelong frown, he added, "Among other things, of course."

She lay her head back on his shoulder, wondering about those other things. Could they possibly be strong enough to make him think about a future with her? Bentley knew that was what she wanted. And what she feared was beyond her reach.

Reid's boundless drive and incessant traveling precluded the kind of traditional relationship most couples enjoyed. During the interminable weeks of separation, she had been forced to accept one important fact. She either had to be content with a limited role in his life or she had to get out before she became completely enthralled by him.

Late one night she'd been reading from a favorite book of poetry when a line leaped off the page, cementing the decision that she'd flirted with all along. *No one worth possessing can be quite possessed.*

There had been no choice, really. Love was stingy with its options. So she would take as much as he would grant her, for as long as she could get it. Maybe it would be enough.

"Why the sigh?" Reid asked, leaning forward so he could see her face.

Bentley avoided his gaze, concentrating instead on the greenish-gray water lapping at the sandy beach. "I was just thinking that life sometimes gives us a great deal more than we have a right to expect . . . and so much less than we hope for."

With faint pressure of his thumb and forefinger, he forced her to look at him. "What is it you want, Bentley, that you can't have?"

"All of you," she said simply. Then, as if the attorney had to defend her position, she jumped to her feet. She paced back and forth in front of him, formulating her argument. "I realize it's naive, childish even, to think that someone like you might consider settling down."

"Why?"

"Why?" His question was so simplistic that she searched for an equally simple answer. "Because you do megadeals in Russia, then jet on over to China and negotiate with government officials for several months."

"So?"

Was the man obtuse? "Reid, men who fly in that

orbit do not deal with mortgage payments, crabgrass, and children's orthodontia.''

"Are you saying that's what *you* want, Bentley?'' He shrugged. "I gotta tell you that surprises me. But if you're set on having 'em, I'll see what I can do.''

Eyes narrowed, she whirled around to confront him. "Don't you dare patronize me, you . . . you . . . tycoon!'' Under normal circumstances she'd have been able to come up with a more imaginative epithet, but this was a sore subject.

"You don't think tycoons bother with the same details as everyone else?''

"They aren't *like* everyone else,'' Bentley said softly, her anger ebbing as quickly as it had flared. "Tycoons don't want, don't need, the same things out of life that other people do.''

Reid must have noticed the rigid set of her shoulders, the protective way she held her arms in front of her beneath the poncho. He tugged her down to the bench again, muttering, "Well, hell. One way or another, you're ruining every one of my plans.''

"You accused me of the same thing last night. Maybe it's time you explained.''

"All the time I was out of the country, I was thinking ahead, planning the details for what I hoped would be a memorable reunion.'' He threw up one hand to halt her interruption. "I know. Last night was pretty damned memorable. But we jumped ahead a few steps.''

"Now I'm really intrigued,'' Bentley said, shifting to look expectantly at him. "What did we miss?''

He counted a point on one index finger. "For starters I was going to take you to someplace special, elegant.

You know, candlelight, hovering waiters, maybe a harp.''

Bentley giggled, then bit her lower lip when he glared. "I'm sorry. Harps simply aren't your style."

He didn't dispute her claim, merely continued reciting his list. "After that I aimed to order the best champagne on the menu and see that you drank just enough to be receptive."

"To what? You had to know how much I wanted you. We both knew the next time we saw each other—"

"I wanted you receptive to what I was going to tell you first. The lovemaking would have come later, when it would have meant even more."

Bentley's heart tapped out a frenzied cadence. She licked her lips and swallowed. Unable to wait any longer, she asked, "What were you going to tell me?"

"That I love you."

"Oh, Reid." Her throat constricted and her eyes filled. He'd told her the best news of her life and her impulse was to cry, which annoyed her. She sniffed.

He rushed on as if eager to get the rest of the story told. "I knew it after holding you all night in New York, but I wanted to—"

"I knew it, too," Bentley said, grasping his hand.

"Knew I loved you?"

"No, I hadn't guessed that. But I knew *I* loved *you*, and I hoped . . ." She touched his face, traced the creases that bracketed his mouth, whisked her fingers over his mustache, but her eyes never strayed from his. "I love you," she said again, giddy with the wonder of its sound.

Then they were securely entwined in each other's arms, repeating the words over and over as if to compensate for all the days they'd been unable to say them.

Bentley wasn't aware that the moisture had escaped from her eyes until Reid pulled back and followed a damp trail down her cheek with his thumb.

"What's this?" he chided softly.

"Tears of joy." She blinked rapidly several times. "I can't believe this is really happening. I wished and dreamed, hoped . . . but I wasn't sure if there was a chance."

"I know. Maybe waiting all those months was a mistake."

"No, no." She shook her head vigorously. "I think it was good for us to endure what we did. It made me even more positive about how I feel." It had also taught her that she could survive long periods away from Reid. "Somehow the waiting, the anticipation, made last night more special."

"Mmm, I guess. But I don't intend to suffer that way again." He stretched out his long legs and tugged her close against his side. "Bet you never guessed that I got so frustrated I started running."

"Cruel and unusual punishment, huh?" she asked, hearing his disgust. "Well, it isn't my fault. I'm not the one who took off for months."

"Don't think I didn't resent every single day I was gone. That will *never* happen again."

Bentley's initial reservations about the kind of future they could have returned with a vengeance. "Reid, I told you before. Don't make promises we both know you can't keep." She lifted his hand and rubbed her thumb over his fingers. "Next time it may not be Russia or China, and it may not be months, but there will be a next time. And probably it will be soon."

"You've conditioned yourself not to expect much from me, haven't you?"

She started at the sharp edge in his voice and searched his expression for its cause. "It's not that so much as that I'm a realist. I have firsthand experience as to what I can expect." It was faint and fleeting, but she saw the regret as it flashed in his eyes, then disappeared.

"Reid, don't misunderstand. I'm not complaining. I told you when you called that I've made my decision. You'll find me surprisingly undemanding."

Bentley winced as yet another of his creative curses stung her ear. "Tough," he grunted. "That isn't the way this works. You have a right to expect—to demand—as much from me as I'm going to take from you."

He fixed a piercing stare on her. "And if you've got some half-baked notion that ours won't be a traditional relationship in every sense of the word, let me set you straight right now. You will not have license to run free just because I happen to go out of town once in a while."

She had to restrain her smile. This was Reid in his element, all sign of complacency gone. "I wasn't suggesting anything of the sort. But our time together will be infrequent and short-lived. By definition, that means there will be limits—"

He told her very succinctly what she could do with limits. "Bentley, don't you know me well enough to understand that when I take on anything, I get *involved*. I jump in with both feet." He grasped both her shoulders. "Which brings up the next point in my plan."

"Ah, yes, the plan. We've had atmosphere, champagne, a confession of love. Have we worked up to the seduction yet?'' Her words were gentle taunts, softened with a smile.

"Nope," he denied smugly. "There's one more step before that."

His lopsided grin was disconcerting, like that of a little boy with a secret. "I can't imagine what."

"Will you marry me?"

"I . . . I . . . what did you say?" Her ears rang, color suffused her face, dizzy spots danced before her vision.

"Dammit, Bentley," he swore, as if her astonishment offended him. "What did you think the next step would be? Isn't this the logical order of things when two people are in love?"

"Y-yes, I suppose s-so," she said, unable to control the stammer. Too many pleasant shocks in one day had left her reeling. "Married."

"Well, will you?"

Reality began to penetrate. "Yes! Of course I will."

"So," he began, taking control like the tycoon he was, "how long will it take to put a wedding together? Now that we've come to an agreement, I don't see any advantage in waiting. I want to move on this ASAP."

Bentley smacked a kiss on his cheek. "Why, Reid, I've never heard anything so romantic. Is this how you operate when you make another acquisition?"

He ducked his head and grinned sheepishly. "Sorry. Guess I got carried away." One hand came up to frame her face. "Sweetheart, if you want romantic, then I'll take my best shot at doing it right. That's a promise."

He stood and pulled her up with him. "I guess we

can talk about plans later. Let's go back and get ready
for our celebration. I probably shouldn't have spilled
the beans about my plans for last night. That way, I
could surprise you with them tonight."

"I'll bet if you really apply your computer brain to
it, you might still pull a few surprises out of your bag
of tricks."

He laughed and gave her a lazy wink that was rife
with sexual promise. "Count on it."

The word atmosphere was inadequate. It didn't begin
to describe Reid's favorite restaurant. He'd lobbied in
favor of taking her out for a fancy meal. Bentley, however, insisted they go where he would have gone had
she not been with him. As he pulled the rental car to
a stop, she couldn't stop gaping at the peeling gold
minaret, perched atop the converted house like a
crooked afterthought.

They skirted a huddle of abandoned refrigerators
and entered a crowded room dominated by a long,
old-fashioned bar. Bentley's eyes watered from the
hazy cloud of smoke, but her taste buds tingled when
she inhaled the redolent aromas of ethnic cooking.
The din of laughter and good-natured arguments were
sure signs of a place where customers enjoyed them-
selves.

An older man waved from behind the bar, and after
serving up several more beers, he came to greet them.
"So," he said in a heavy accent, "you don't call until
late. I still save you the best table."

He shook hands with Reid, but his gaze rested on
Bentley. "You teach this boy some manners, eh?"
the gray-haired proprietor advised after they'd been
introduced. "He brings his giants up from Houston

to beat our team." His mouth puckered and he made a series of reproving sounds. "But Mama, she don't know basketball. She say she'll cook for him anyway."

He steered them across a worn linoleum floor to the only vacant table, and with a flourish, seated them in mismatched chairs. Signaling one of the scurrying waitresses, he spoke to Bentley while eyeing her critically. "I hope you got a big appetite. You don't look like you eat enough dumplings."

He hurried back to the bar, leaving her shaking her head. No haughty maître d' here, and the incessant clanging of an ancient cash register supplied the only music. She examined the teapot converted to a lamp which adorned their scratched-Formica table, then transferred her attention to the truly ugly still life food posters that served as wall decor.

"You hate it," Reid said when the jangling finally ceased and conversation became easier. "I knew you would. I tried to warn you."

Bentley laughed at his dismay. "It's wonderful. This is just the sort of place I love to find when I travel. I'll bet the food is outstanding."

"I think so. The family is Serbian and everyone who works here is related. Mama cooks, Papa tends bar, their three sons divide the business end of things, and the daughters-in-law wait tables.

Papa descended on them again bearing two bottles of Bip beer, concentrating as he poured them into glasses. Bentley toasted Reid's with hers. "Here's to celebrations."

"It's not champagne, but be careful. This is strong stuff." He took a taste and Bentley followed suit.

Papa helped himself to one of the empty chairs. "So,

what you gonna feed your missus?" he asked, leaning forward to peer at the scoop of goat's cheese and home-made bread their waitress had just delivered. Then he nodded approvingly at Reid. "About time you found one and settled down."

Bentley smiled at the term "missus" and at the un-abashed meddling. Since Reid was also smiling, she supposed the subject of his marital status had been dis-cussed before.

"His poor mama and papa," the old man lamented, pointing a censuring finger at Reid. "Four children they raised, three of them fine, big sons, and only two little ones to show for it." He shook his head in sympathy for the unfortunate Hunters. "And me." He touched his heart. "Blessed with so many."

As if to emphasize his good fortune, a small army of children streaked across the room in pursuit of a calico cat. Most of the patrons paid little attention to the chase scene. It apparently happened often.

"Well, I got to get back. My boy there," he said, indicating a man preparing to tune up the cash register again, "he says, 'Papa, you mind everybody's business but your own.' I ask you, do I do such a thing?" Without waiting for a reply, he went back to his post at the bar.

Bentley said, "Wow," and took another sip of her beer. "Maybe I ought to pump him some more. He seems to know things about your family that you never told me."

Reid shrugged. "Guess it never came up. When I'm around you, talking about family is the farthest thing from my mind."

His look left no doubt as to what was on his mind right then. Bentley felt a warm flush spread over her.

Reid had been right—they had waited so long that one night wasn't going to come close to being enough. Then she remembered. They had the rest of their lives.

"I love you," she whispered, stretching over to touch his cheek. He covered her hand, and after looking at her for a long, tender interval, he turned to brush the lightest of kisses over her palm.

The mood was shattered when the kitchen door flew open revealing a glimpse of a woman bent over the stove sampling from a pan while her other hand held firmly to a cane. Before she could comment on the woman's dedication, their table was being loaded with platters of tempting food.

Spanokopita, chicken paprikash with dumplings, goulash, moussaka . . . the array was endless. "I couldn't decide what I liked best," Reid admitted, "so I told them to bring some of most everything. I wanted you to try them all."

While various family members bustled back and forth, Bentley sampled, approved, and complimented one delicious Serbian creation after another. Like Reid, she was hard-pressed to choose a favorite. "Yummm," she said, in ecstasy after her first taste of the baklava they had for dessert. "This is the best I've ever had anywhere, including Greece."

Much later, in the Elephant Room of the Milwaukee Athletic Club, Bentley confessed, "I don't think I'll ever eat again. Those people take food seriously."

She and Reid had driven back to the club in near-silence. Since his arrival last night, so much had happened to link them that at times conversation seemed redundant. Bentley was so aware of him, so in tune with him that words weren't necessary.

Since Reid wouldn't let himself be diverted entirely from his original intentions, which included celebrating their engagement with champagne, they had stopped by the Elephant Room for the ritual.

He puffed on a surprisingly good-smelling cigar that he'd picked up at the tobacconist shop in the lobby. "I've never seen you smoke or drink before," Bentley said, taking her first swallow of the impressive French champagne. "And here in one evening you've had a Bip beer, plus a glass of champagne and a cigar."

"The only thing you need to worry about is that I probably won't sleep all night. That's how alcohol affects me."

She strove to appear nonchalant by snuggling in her comfortable chair and gazing at the life-size elephants adorning the wallpaper. The entire club was overwhelmingly masculine—women were allowed only as guests of male members. Rather than being outraged by the sexism, Bentley found the place and its traditions charming. "I should worry that you won't sleep? All night?"

"Worry may not be the operative word." The gleam in his eyes was altogether too naughty. "But then, maybe sleep isn't, either."

It was inexcusable to gulp Dom Pérignon, and foolish to let his innuendo make her turn hot all over. "I thought we were going to discuss plans," she said to mask her growing excitement.

"Ah, yes. Plans." Reid drained his glass and very precisely set it back on the table. "This is how I see it. I want a traditional wedding with family and friends—lots of them—as witnesses. And traditional vows, not ones we make up to suit us."

Bentley knew she should inject her own opinions so he didn't get the mistaken idea that everything would be done his way. But so far, she couldn't disagree with either of his wishes.

"I want us to be husband and wife in the old-fashioned sense of the word, no quibbling about what those terms mean. We won't be going in separate directions independent of each other, both of us pursuing individual goals to the exclusion of our marriage. We need to agree on that here and now."

He was certainly playing the heavy-handed autocrat on this issue. At the same time, his attitude conformed to her own views down the line. Still, he needn't believe she would let him get by with dictating all the terms.

"Your lifestyle doesn't lend itself to that type of relationship," she pointed out reasonably. "I think we'd both better come to terms with that before we go any further."

His brows drew together in one dark, heavy line. "I've been on the road a lot of years, and I've enjoyed it. I guess I always saw myself as a modern-day adventurer, tilting at windmills, taking on the big boys, and I've had a fine time doing it all."

Yes, that sounded like her Reid, the man she'd chosen to love. For better or worse.

"But I don't need to be quite as much of a crusader as I was in the early days, don't need to prove so much. I've done most of what I wanted to. In fact, I'm in a position to do whatever I damned well please, including sit on my front porch and swat flies."

Bentley couldn't hold in her mirthful laugh at the image of that. She doubted if Reid would last one day engaged in such sedentary pursuits. "Don't you think you'd get bored with a more routine pace?"

"I'm ready for a change. I want you and a home, time to get away to the beach house for long weekends."

"Oh, Reid," she exclaimed, "I adore that house. I can't explain why, but I felt right at home the minute I drove up. Wait till you see how sensational it looks now." She hurriedly filled him in on all she'd done.

"Whoa," he said, beaming at her enthusiasm. "Save the rest until you can show me in person. I'll be pretty tied up the first couple of weeks back in the office. After that, I'll wind things down so we can be together more."

The bar was quiet and Reid was speaking so softly Bentley had to lean close to hear him. "Tonight at the restaurant, while Papa was giving his lecture, it hit me why I bought that Victorian monstrosity in the Heights. I didn't realize until I met you that I want to make it a home. I want us to be a family in every way, and that includes children. I'm prepared to do whatever's necessary to have that."

She felt her eyes go misty at hearing his commitment to her and a family. But as he'd said, he always got enthusiastic about any new venture. He'd also admitted to losing interest once he'd accomplished what he set out to do. Undaunted, she made up her mind to be the one project that continued to fascinate him. There were ways . . .

She yawned delicately and looked at him through lowered lids. Reid didn't mistake the message, grinning as he stood and latched onto her arm.

In the elevator, Bentley asked in her most seductive voice, "Your room or mine?"

"You're a liberated lady. I think I'd like it a lot if you came to me."

Bentley did just that, after a short detour by her room. And much later she fell asleep in Reid's arms knowing that no day in her life would ever rival the perfection of this one.

ELEVEN

It was the worst day of her life.

Clutching the treacherous report, Bentley battled a rising tide of nausea. She'd never fainted, but that might be another first, on a day that had already produced one too many.

She flung the binder to her desk, as if the report itself were lethal. Yet there was no way she could keep from rereading the contemptible words.

"This can't be," she whispered tremulously, seeking a way to negate the far-reaching impact of what she'd just learned. But as a lawyer, she couldn't escape the truth.

Permanently assigned to the contracts department, she'd been given the information on this deal, a straightforward account of how a group of partners began by purchasing approximately eight percent of a company's stock as an investment. More stock had been accumulated; takeover became the obvious goal. The next step—pending—would be a cash tender offer for just over fifty percent of the company.

On the surface there was nothing to distinguish this transaction from countless others.

In reality, it was an attempt by Reid Hunter and some partners to steal Bill Rutledge's lifeblood, the cruelest kind of deceit Bentley could imagine. She would not stand for it! "I'll see you in hell first, Renegade!"

Fury stormed in to replace the initial debilitating numbness. She snatched up the file and charged out of her office. She had no plan beyond confronting Reid and demanding an explanation. Surely he would confirm that this was simply a misunderstanding. After all, he loved her.

Bentley's heels clicked down the tiled corridor, each step closer to his office reinforcing her determination. It had to be a mistake. Otherwise, she'd been betrayed by the most important person in her life.

Disregarding protocol, she sailed right by Marian, pretending she was entering a courtroom to prosecute a case. She made it halfway across the room before Reid's welcoming smile faded to a wary frown. "You can't go through with this," she said.

"What?" he asked, eyeing the folder she waved at him.

"The deal you've been working on." Bentley's confidence grew when she heard her voice, cool and detached. A good start. "You have to call it off."

His forehead wrinkled and he watched her for a few seconds before reaching over to nab the file. "Ah, Willco. I didn't know you'd be working on this one."

"No, I don't imagine you did. As you can see, I am. And I'm asking you to give up the attempted takeover." Hearing emotion start to creep into her voice, she paused and took a breath before finishing. "You must stop it."

"With all due respect, Bentley, that's not a request you get to make."

She wanted to scream at him, accuse him of duplicity, of using her as a pawn. Instead, she invoked her trial skills to keep herself under control. "Oh, really? Whom do you think has a more legitimate right to make the request?"

He sat back and regarded her with half-closed eyes. "Don't tell me you're going to be one of those women who meddles in her husband's business."

When she heard the amused condescension, Bentley's hard-won control nearly snapped. She gritted her teeth and held on. "I could not care less about any other business decision you will ever make. But I have to insist that you not proceed with the Willco takeover."

"The takeover will proceed as planned."

She'd heard that hard-edged steel in his tone often. It meant, discussion closed. She couldn't accept that, even if it meant begging. "Reid, please. I'm asking you to give it up."

"Not possible," he said, snapping the binder shut, daring her to argue. "It's a done deal."

"Not even for me?" She hated pleading, yet saw no alternative. "I promise I'll never ask another thing of you, but if you love me, you'll do this. One time."

He exhaled a huge sigh and massaged his chin. "What you're trying is called blackmail, you know. I don't think people in love are supposed to do that to each other."

"Then you won't stop the takeover?"

"Even if I were so inclined, which I'm not, I couldn't. There are partners, financing agreements, a hundred other details. This is the big time. You know I can't just suddenly back out. You're not that naive."

Bentley planted both palms on the cherry surface of his desk. "It appears that I'm incredibly naive." She fell back on sarcasm to conceal the hurt. "Why else would I have fallen into your bed so readily, swallowing every one of your lies about a future?"

"What the hell are you talking about?" he roared, leaping to his feet. "I've never lied to you. *Never!*"

"How can you say that? Every kiss, every vow of love was just another piece of your plot to take Willco."

His fingers speared into his disheveled hair. She watched him fight for patience. "Spit it out, Bentley. You're making serious accusations. But I've missed a connection somewhere. What does Willco have to do with us?"

By now her hands were shaking so badly that she clasped them together and pressed them to her stomach. "Don't tell me you don't know who the principal stockholders are."

"It's in the report. William T. and Victoria Brighton Rutledge."

"My mother and stepfather."

"Christ Almighty!" His face paled and he fell back into his chair, the jerky motions mute testament to his shock. "Bentley, honey, I swear I didn't know."

"Don't call me that, damn you! It's all an act." She couldn't let herself trust anything he said or did. Ever.

"Bentley," he said, rising again to stride around the desk. "I know this has upset you, but try to calm down so we can talk reasonably about it." His tone was low and soothing, though tight from the underlying strain.

For every step he took, Bentley moved back one, until he halted his advance. "You expect reason when you've just blown my whole life to bits, demolished my future?" If she didn't get away from him the tears would start. And then he'd see just how vulnerable she was. Her laugh was short and bitter. "Afraid I'm not that magnanimous, Mr. Hunter."

Reid shoved his hands into his pockets and hunched his shoulders forward while he stared at the rug. When their gazes locked again, Bentley hardened herself against the plea she saw in his eyes. She could not let feelings influence her at this point.

There was going to be a fight, and she might as well accept that it would be long and unpleasant with Reid as the enemy.

He took a single cautious step and extended his hand. "Sit down, Bentley. We'll work something out between us."

"There is nothing to work out. The only thing I have left to do here is hand in my resignation. I'll even be civilized and list the reason as conflict of interest rather than what we know it really is."

"Which is?"

She chose the most vulgar, sexually explicit definition in her vocabulary, words that rivaled Reid at his crudest. Bentley was pleased when his face turned a livid red.

"You can't honestly believe I used you that way."

"Why not? For months you've been scheming to take over my stepfather's company, and for months you've been leading me on. You're good, I must admit. You actually had me convinced that you cared for me when all you wanted was an inside source."

"Good Lord," he breathed. "This is too much."

"You even took it further than necessary." *Watch it. You're starting to rave.* "The love and marriage bit was definitely above and beyond the call. I was hot enough to jump into the sack without the flowery promises.''

Reid was on her before she got out the last word, his fingers biting into her arms as he shook her several times. ''I won't listen to that kind of talk. We did not jump into the sack,'' he said savagely. ''We made love, and all your glib words and accusations won't change or cheapen it.'' He shook her again for emphasis. ''We made love.''

''You don't know the meaning of the word.'' All at once the anger drained from her, leaving only sadness and futility. Her eyes burned. Tears edged closer to the surface, ready. She retreated, summoning her remaining strength for a closing argument.

''I hope the prize is worth what this is going to cost you, Mr. Hunter. But let me give you fair warning. I'm going to battle you to the end. You will not get your hands on Willco . . . or me. Ever. You'll rue the day you came up with the bright idea to buy yourself an oil company.''

He said it softly, too late for her to hear. ''I already do.''

Bentley was gone, leaving him with nothing of her but the vividly colored scarf which had slipped from her shoulder when he tried to keep her from leaving him.

He might have been standing there holding the scarf for a minute or an hour when Marian stuck her head inside the door. ''Reid, should I go after Bentley? I think she was crying. Oh, dear. Are you all right?''

He nodded, not looking at her. Then he wandered to his desk, in a fog, incapable of coherent thought.

"I don't mean to pry. I just thought Bentley might need me. She doesn't strike me as the crying type."

"I guess with provocation, anyone is the type to cry." *Tears of joy*. She'd called them that in Milwaukee right after he'd told her he loved her. And less than two weeks later, he'd given her another reason to cry, one that there was virtually no way to defend.

He crumpled into his chair, exhausted. "She needs some time," he reasoned, as much to himself as to Marian. "I'll check on her later."

The eternal optimist, he thought with black humor as his secretary closed the door. He was sure Bentley wouldn't speak to him, much less listen to an explanation of his role in the Willco debacle. She had a right to be angry. Maybe he could even understand why she'd accused him of taking advantage of her. That was the anger talking. But she was wrong. Somehow he had to find a way of proving it to her.

He hadn't lied about his inability to halt the takeover. Too many others were involved; binding legal commitments had been made. Reid propped his forehead on one palm and closed his eyes. But he couldn't obliterate the image of Bentley pleading with him. She had such pride and she'd sacrificed it to him.

"Damm it to hell!" He pounded his desk. Didn't she know he'd give her anything—everything—within his power? Including a multi-million-dollar deal? he asked himself. Because of a woman? Yes, there was no question. No company in the world was worth a single one of her tears. But since he *couldn't* call a halt, he had to find another solution.

He began weighing his options. Her resignation could stand for a while. They could reevaluate her position after the takeover was completed. He didn't fault her for siding with Bill Rutledge. Family loyalty was an admirable trait. When she became his wife, Reid would expect the same loyalty.

But his top priority had nothing to do with business. The first thing he had to do was make her believe in his love, see that his desire for marriage was sincere.

If he called her, she'd hang up for sure. If he showed up on her doorstep, she'd slam the door in his face. So how was he going to get close enough to plead his case? His gaze settled on the desktop appointment calendar, and Reid smiled. Here was a ready-made solution to his problem, handed to him like a gift from the Fates.

After cleaning out her desk at Maverick, Bentley stopped by the house where she'd grown up instead of going to her own home. She went straight to the backyard where she knew she'd find her mother in the gazebo. With few exceptions, Victoria spent several hours there each afternoon working on a needlepoint stair runner.

It was unusually hot for October, and the sun beating down on her reminded Bentley of a similar day five months ago. The day she'd met Reid. Ironically, their first meeting had been much like today's—conflict, confrontation, challenge. Why had she fallen for the illusion that there could ever be more between them?

She skirted the pool and cabana, following a trail of slate stepping-stones to the gazebo where Fashion azeleas bloomed a deep shade of coral.

"Oh, hello, darling," Victoria chirped, smiling between stitches. "Did you leave work early to get ready for our big evening?"

Bentley froze. She'd forgotten. The big evening was

to have been the introduction of Reid to her family and a special dinner followed by the announcement of their engagement to her mother and stepfather. They had planned to repeat the ceremony in Indianapolis next weekend with the Hunters. Now there was no cause for celebration. "No, Mother. I'm afraid there's been a change of plans."

"Oh, I see." Victoria secured her needle in the canvas. "Well, we can always work around that."

Those who didn't know her well might describe Victoria Rutledge as flighty, probably because of her sprightly way of moving and talking, or her ingenuous talent for charming everyone she met. But the surface fluff camouflaged a most organized and detail-oriented mind. Given a purpose, it was impossible to deter Victoria. "What's the problem?" she asked, laying aside her handwork. "Does it have something to do with your young man?"

In spite of her desolation, Bentley managed a weak smile at the old-fashioned term. She sobered instantly. Reid wasn't hers. Never had been, really. Except in her dreams. "Mother, when will Bill get home? I want to tell you both at once."

"I expect him any minute. He called nearly an hour ago to say he was leaving." There was a moment of silence before Victoria's soft voice coaxed, "Bentley, sit down and tell me what's wrong. I've never seen you look so upset."

Standing had sapped her strength, and Bentley sagged onto one of the gazebo's floral cushions. She looked at her mother through a watery veil, then told herself not to waste any more tears. At the sound of heavy boots clumping down the walkway, she sat up straight and steeled herself.

"Here are my two best girls." Bill bent to kiss Victoria, then Bentley. "Figured you ladies would be primping for the big 'do' tonight." His wife silenced him with an almost imperceptible shake of her head.

Bentley knew she couldn't delay any longer so she stood and motioned Bill to take her place. "For the past five months, ever since I went to work at Maverick Enterprises, Reid Hunter has been pursuing me." Ignoring the anxious looks on her parents' faces, she went on. "At first I resisted, but he is . . . well, Reid. In short, I fell in love and rather foolishly believed that he had, too."

"Reid Hunter is the man you're bringing to dinner tonight?" Victoria and Bill voiced the question in unison.

"*Was* the man. He won't be coming after all." She bit her lip, then forced out the rest. "Just as we won't be announcing our engagement."

"Engagement!" Bill blustered.

"Why?" Victoria asked.

Bentley laughed, a brittle sound that had nothing to do with humor. "Because today I found out it was all a ruse. He was using me to expedite one of the deals he's so famous for."

"Used you in what way?" Bill demanded through gritted teeth. He sat rigid, as if prepared to attack.

"It turns out you had good reason for those nagging suspicions you've had recently." The next part would be the worst. "Reid Hunter, along with a group of partners, plan to take over Willco. They've been planning it for months. I was just a convenient dupe."

"The hell you say!"

"Well, of all things."

Oddly enough, it was Victoria who swore and Bill

who sounded disbelieving. Equally surprising was the fact that Victoria jumped up and took charge. "Let me get this straight. What did Hunter do to make you think he used you as a dupe?"

"Mo-ther," Bentley protested impatiently. "That's the least of our problems. Didn't you hear the word takeover?"

"Of course I did. There's nothing wrong with my hearing. Answer the question. How did he use you?"

"He deceived me, kept his maneuverings a secret all the time he was se—courting me," she snapped, annoyed that she'd stumbled over the word seduced. "But that isn't the issue now."

"Indulge me, dear, because I think it *is* the issue." Victoria looked at Bill as if to say "let me handle this," and his silence gave her permission. "Did he at any time ask you specific questions about Willco?"

Bentley thought back over the many conversations she'd had with Reid and could only remember two occasions when he'd mentioned an oil company. Once, he'd asked her how she would advise him to acquire one, the other time, he had said he'd visited some offshore rigs. Paltry evidence for an indictment.

"No, he never asked for specifics about Willco. However, that doesn't change the fact that he's going to take it over. Mother, don't you see? He's the enemy. Why are you looking for a way to defend him?" Unable to contain her vexation any longer, she began pacing.

"I'm hardly defending him," Victoria pointed out, growing calmer as her daughter's agitation increased. "But I should think an attorney would want to take all the facts into account."

"The one salient fact we need to keep in mind is

that Reid and his buddies want to boot Bill out of his own company." She glanced at her curiously silent stepfather and wondered why he hadn't exploded.

"Of course that is important," Victoria conceded. "And we'll have to deal with it later. But first, can you say for certain that Reid even knew you were related to Bill?"

Again Bentley searched her memory and had to admit that she and Reid hadn't spent much time discussing their families. They'd always been too wrapped up in each other. "Since our last names are different, I suppose it's possible that he didn't know," she allowed grudgingly. "I read the complete file and Rutledge was the only name included."

Like a dog with a bone, Victoria persisted. "Think, Bentley. Was there ever a single instance where he *used* you as a pipeline to Willco?"

She didn't have to think. Completely demoralized by her mother's arguments, Bentley plopped back down on the cushions. She saw her reaction for what it was— a shield against the agony of having to give up Reid. Knowing she had to ally herself with Bill, she'd sought a way of turning Reid into a villain.

"All right, so what if he didn't use our relationship to his own advantage? What does that prove?"

"Why, just this, darling," Victoria said with a satisfied smile. "I know you, and you'd never fall in love with a man who isn't worthy of that love." She sat down and took Bill's hand. "Keep that in mind and I'm sure everything will work out, including this nasty business of the takeover."

"Oh, Mother," Bentley wailed. Victoria was the proverbial Pollyanna when her family's happiness was at stake. "You're such a hopeless romantic."

Victoria looked pleased, as if she'd been paid the ultimate compliment. "When one is a romantic, dear, nothing is ever hopeless."

"You must be Mrs. Rutledge. It's easy to see why Bentley's so gorgeous."

"I do not believe this!" Bentley fumed when she heard the too-familiar gravelly voice drift in from the foyer. Her mother had gone to answer the doorbell, leaving Bill and Bentley in the library.

"And, of course, you're Reid Hunter," Victoria's soft, captivating voice replied.

Fire in her eyes, Bentley headed for the entry hall to rescue her mother. She stopped short in the double doorway. Lord, would she ever be able to see him and not feel his potency all the way to her bones? For the hundredth time she told herself he wasn't good-looking, and as usual, ended up admitting that no other man had even come close to fascinating her as Reid did. *Put it behind you*!

"What are you doing here?" she challenged, crossing her arms as she leaned against the door facing, adopting his pose of choice.

"I was invited to dinner. At six-thirty, I believe."

As if consorting with Reid, an antique clock beside Bentley chimed the half hour. She felt like kicking it. On second thought, why not kick the interloper standing there with a self-satisfied grin on his face?

"For you," he said, bending slightly to hand a showy bouquet of roses to Victoria. "Looks like I chose the right color."

"How lovely," Victoria gushed. "Bentley, isn't this a marvelous shade of coral? And look, they're a perfect match for my dress."

"Perfect," Bentley grumbled peevishly, watching her mother accept the flowers. She'd never seen roses that shade and wondered where he'd found them. It irritated her that the color was unique, and that two dozen seemed just the right number. Mildly extravagant, but not ostentatious.

"And this," Reid said, holding up a champagne bottle, "is for the toast later." He and Victoria traded smiles that looked overly chummy to Bentley.

"Too bad you won't be here later," she informed him haughtily, plucking the bottle from his hand. "But I'll be sure to remember you in our toast. Nothing will give me more pleasure than drinking to your downfall with Dom Pérignon that your money bought."

"Bentley!" her mother scolded, touching Reid's arm to draw him deeper into the foyer. "Mind your manners. Mr. Hunter is a guest."

"Reid, ma'am."

"Oh, my God," Bentley muttered under her breath. "Now he's talking like John Wayne. So help me if he swaggers, I *will* kick him."

"Reid, then. And you must call me Victoria. Let's go into the library. We were just about to have a before-dinner drink."

Bentley couldn't detect a swagger, but this farce had gone on long enough. She slithered her way in front of the pair. "Don't be ridiculous, Mother. He can't stay." Unfortunately, there wasn't enough of her to completely obstruct the wide entrance.

"Of course he can, darling. After all, you did invite him. It would be inexcusably bad form to renege on an invitation. Besides, Delia's making hazelnut steak."

Victoria smiled up at her escort in silent collusion, leaving Bentley to wonder when her mother had become so feeble she couldn't walk without holding on to a man's arm. Hearing Bill come up behind her, she ground her teeth and refused to budge.

"This man is a traitor," Bentley charged. "As we stand here, he's plotting to take over our company." Only yesterday, she'd had no interest in Willco. Now circumstances had thrust her into the role of protector.

"I was hoping we could talk about that," Reid said evenly, denying nothing.

"See there. I told you this afternoon that everything would turn out fine," Victoria reminded Bentley. "But I insist we don't talk business tonight. We've more important things on the agenda."

Reid nodded in agreement and reached past Bentley to hand a box to Bill. "Mr. Rutledge, someone told me you like a cigar now and then. These are some of the best."

"Hmmph," Bentley grunted, seeing her stepfather accept the offering after a moment's hesitation. Reid was really laying on the charm with a trowel. Why didn't Bill simply order the big fake out of his house?

"Bill, darling," Victoria said, giving her husband a smile that Bentley knew reduced him to silly putty. He couldn't refuse her anything. "Fix Reid a drink."

"He doesn't drink. It keeps him awake all night." She snapped her mouth shut so fast, her teeth rattled. And Reid, damn him, had the audacity to grin at her with wicked familiarity.

"I'll have whatever you're having, sir," he said, gesturing at Bill's bourbon and water.

"Oh, brother. I give up." Bentley had muttered, grumbled, and grunted enough in the past ten minutes to last her a lifetime. It promised to get worse. Victoria had prevailed and Reid would be staying for dinner.

She'd led the two men into the library after ordering Bentley to tell Delia that they would eat in thirty minutes.

Bentley registered her objection by spending the entire half hour in the kitchen with Delia, watching her prepare the hazelnut steak. Too bad she had to share the heavenly veal dish with that viper.

"I don't think I've ever tasted anything better than this," the viper commented a short time later after sampling his first bite of the meat with its light coating of ground nuts and hollandaise sauce.

Victoria alternated a beatific smile between her daughter and their guest. "It's Bentley's favorite, too. She always insists we have it on special occasions."

He nodded and took another bite. Bentley's mouth went dry when she watched him chew. She had to wet her lips when he swallowed. And when he looked at her, her fork clattered onto her plate. His eyes were hot, so hot, and she felt fire spread over every inch of her.

"Tonight is very special," he said in that gritty voice that transformed her into a brainless bundle of yearning.

Bentley took a huge gulp of wine. *Don't let him get to you this way.* Her glass clinked when she set it down too forcefully. Several drops splashed onto Victoria's best lace tablecloth. Reid's fault, she consoled herself.

Throughout the remainder of the meal, Bentley kept her mouth shut unless someone asked her a question. And when Victoria would have herded them back to the library for coffee, she put her foot down. Maybe Bill couldn't stop his wife from orchestrating this mockery, but she'd had enough.

She got a firm grip on Reid's arm and steered him

toward the front door. "Mr. Hunter can't stay. He's already taken too much time away from his business."

Neither Reid nor Victoria put up an argument, and while that made Bentley suspicious, she wasn't inclined to question even the smallest blessing. She watched agape as Reid offered a handshake to Bill, who reluctantly returned it. Then he bent low and brushed Victoria's cheek, telling her what a pleasure it was to meet her, thanking her for the lovely evening, promising he'd see them soon.

As if she had hold of a rag doll, Bentley jerked him out the door. "An amusing little scene, Mr. Hunter. I hope you enjoyed yourself because things are about to go downhill in a hurry."

"Actually, I did enjoy myself. All things considered, tonight went surprisingly well. Better than I expected."

"Surprisingly well?" It was difficult to keep cool in the face of such outrageous behavior. "I can't imagine what you hoped to accomplish by coming here."

"To meet your family. Which I did. To make them like me, which I did . . . halfway. To make our engagement official by giving you a ring. Which I will."

"Are you insane, you . . . you . . . steamroller?"

"No," he said, the soul of sanity and reason. "I am neither insane nor a steamroller." He came at her like one, though. "What I am, is very determined."

"Reid, stay away from me," Bentley warned, inching back. "This is too bizarre for words. We're at war. Shouldn't even be talking to each other."

"Talk isn't what interests me right now." He snagged her wrist and with little effort, pulled her into him.

He struck so fast, so unexpectedly, that he was well into the kiss and Bentley was well into responding before she remembered to fight him. By then it was too late. His mouth was masterful, his embrace restricting, and his body generous with its secrets. Contrary to everything prohibiting it, Bentley wanted him with sudden desperation.

Before she was fully aware of the implications, Reid had pulled away and was holding one of her hands. Distracted by the fervor of his kiss, it took her a few seconds to realize he'd slipped a ring onto her finger.

"No! I can't take this!" But neither could she take it off. He had bent her fingers closed, holding them so she could do nothing but stare hypnotized at the stone, struck by the beauty of the thing.

Flanked by two brilliant-cut diamonds, the emerald was huge and so alive with color and light that it glittered even in the dimness of the gas lamps. Bentley shook her head and looked up at Reid, silently imploring him not to torture her this way.

"It's yours. Just as I am. And you'll never get rid of either of us." After another fiery kiss, he bounded down the steps, leaving Bentley to stare at the Porsche's departing taillights.

"I gotta give you credit, Hunter. Coming here took more guts than any man ought to have."

Inside the house, Bill and Victoria sipped brandy, each lost in their own quiet thoughts. At last Bill broke the silence with a wry assessment. "I'll say one thing . . . that young man has solid brass *cojones*."

"Well, of course he does, darling. That's why he's the perfect man for Bentley."

TWELVE

Bentley unfolded the morning paper and laid it on her patio table, but the headlines held no interest. She was too preoccupied with the blazing emerald on her left hand. Since Reid had forced it on to her finger last night, she'd taken it off a hundred times, only to replace it again.

As angry as she wanted to be at him, as badly as she wanted to despise him, she still admired his style. What other man would be so brash as to show up for his engagement party on the same day his fiancée discovered that he planned to take over her family's company. No one but Reid.

Not only had he shown up, he'd bluffed his way through the entire evening as if he had every right to be there. He'd appeared on time, bearing gifts and sporting his best company manners. He'd had his hair cut and styled, the first time she had known him to make the effort. His suit was new, conservatively tailored and expensive. She'd never seen him look better.

Bentley guessed his game plan right away. He meant

189

to win over Victoria and Bill, then move on to her. Her mother had quickly succumbed to his charm, the two of them thick as thieves. At least Bill had been less forthcoming with his acceptance, though not as indignant as the situation demanded. She couldn't figure out why.

Victoria was transparent. She, with her fanciful idea that romance could cure every ill, believed that if Bentley and Reid trusted their feelings, the problems concerning Willco would disappear. Her mother loved happy endings and made it her mission to ensure them as often as possible. She was doomed to failure in this particular story.

A cloud rolled away from the sun and the emerald tantalized her again. Bentley extended her arm full length, turning her hand side to side to watch the play of sunlight through the stone. How had he known?

She rarely wore jewelry and never rings. But she'd always harbored a secret penchant for emeralds. Reid's was magnificent. At least five carats, it was a true green with no tinges of blue or yellow to mar its color, and it had few of the pervasive flaws so typical of the stone.

She'd have to send it back, of course. First thing Monday she would contact a messenger service. Until then, perhaps she could be forgiven for needing to wear it.

There was a meeting scheduled in an hour, one in which they would try to devise a strategy to thwart Reid. She would wear the ring to remind her of his treachery.

They'd had only two weeks of being truly together, secure in the knowledge of shared feelings. If she had known him longer, loved him better, would this parting have been even more devastating? Bentley found it hard to imagine being more wretched than she was now.

But she couldn't wallow in despair, not when Bill needed her strength and support. She could remember her father, Elliott North, who'd died when she was ten. But Bill had been there when she'd learned to drive, had her first date, gone off to college. He'd given her unreserved love and acceptance and loyalty. She owed him the same.

And to give him that meant waging war on the man she loved.

Bentley stood at one end of a large table, facing a hastily convened assembly of Willco's board of directors. Considering that most of them had been summoned late Friday afternoon, it was a miracle that all twelve were available.

She and Bill had stayed up until the wee hours setting the agenda for today's session. He had requested that she present the issues to the board, insisting she'd be able to spell out their options more clearly than he could. He'd never made any secret that he preferred exploration and production to management. Wild Bill Rutledge was a wildcatter at heart. He had little stomach for corporate machinations, preferring to leave that to his managers. Until now, it had been an arrangement that had worked well.

Bentley spoke with authority, once again grateful for her years of experience in court. "Our first action needs to be a postponement of the annual stockholders' meeting, which is scheduled in two weeks." She saw several nods. "That way we make sure the takeover directors can't be elected."

The delay was unanimously agreed on. Bentley

hadn't had a chance to poll the members as to where they stood regarding the takeover. Regardless of their individual stances, collectively they knew Willco had to buy time.

"I'm sure none of you needs to have our alternatives spelled out. We've all witnessed plenty of these raids before. But let's just clarify them."

She went to an easel and wrote a single word with a bold black marker. "Suitor. We can court a friendly one, a company that might agree to terms which aren't singularly detrimental to us." She drew double lines under the word. "Not an ideal solution, but it would foil the hostile bunch."

By number two she made a dollar sign. "We can buy back large blocks of stock at a premium in order to retain control. Thanks to conservative management, we are in a position to do this, though it would leave us crippled from a financial standpoint, fair game, so to speak. And we don't want to go through this again."

A murmur of dismay went around the table. Bentley figured that would be the first option ruled out. "Or . . ." She sketched a cannon by number three. "We can declare all-out war on the raiders. There's no question we'll get bloodied in the process, but at least it'll send them a message that we won't go down without a fight."

She had armed herself for battle and didn't plan to even suggest the possibility of negotiating with the invaders in hopes they might win a few concessions.

Bentley didn't want crumbs from Reid Hunter. Maybe he hadn't purposely used her, but the end result was the same. And she wanted him to pay for it. The emerald weighed heavily on her hand.

At the end of a long, tedious day, when all the

choices had been painstakingly debated, the only accord they'd reached was to pursue each option further and meet again in one week.

In the intervening time, Bentley and Bill huddled with executives from the five companies that had been designated as possible suitors. Sandwiched between those meetings were consultations with experts on acquisitions and mergers, plus discussions with stockholders who voted enough shares to influence the final outcome.

Facts, figures, and scenarios circled through her brain in a continuous loop. The first volley of the war had barely been fired and already Bentley felt shell-shocked. She told herself she had to keep going, maintain an optimistic front for Bill's sake.

He had not yet reacted with the outrage and resentment that would have been expected and appropriate under the circumstances. Instead he seemed detached, as if he had more important matters to consider. So Bentley worked harder to compensate.

At the second board meeting she convinced a majority of members that Willco could fight the takeover successfully. Once she'd accomplished that, she plunged into the task of securing adequate financial backing to see them through. It wasn't easy.

Sometimes in the darkest hours, before dawn brought another arduous day, she gave in to self-pity. It seemed as though the entire burden of opposing Reid had fallen on her shoulders. She began to question the accuracy of his initial assessment of her—that she didn't know how to fight for what she wanted. What if he were right. . . .

If Bentley's actions were frenzied, and Bill's half-hearted, Victoria never wavered in her goal to preserve normalcy at home. When Bentley wasn't out of town, her mother insisted she come there for dinner. Tonight, she'd invited several relatives and friends, and wouldn't give up until she had turned Bentley's no to a yes. So here she sat, wishing she'd made her refusal stick.

"Beer for you, Adrian, and mineral water for the little mother," Steve Willis said, carrying drinks from the bar.

"I don't think I'll ever be little again," Beth bemoaned, giving her huge stomach a mournful look. Bentley's pregnant cousin and her husband, Adrian, along with Adrian's partner Steve, had no doubt been summoned by Victoria to liven things up.

"Sure I can't get you a drink, Bentley?" Steve asked.

She blinked and pulled her gaze away from the snapping flames in the fireplace. "What? Oh, no, I'm fine." *Liar!* She was miserable. But not miserable enough to miss the exchanged looks of concern between everyone in the room.

Bentley pasted a smile on her face and directed it at the man at the bar. "Thanks, Steve, but I'll pass."

"Just whistle if you change your mind."

She had always thought of Steve Willis as a perfectly likable guy. He'd been a guest so frequently in the past few years that he was almost like family. But tonight he seemed just a little too short, his voice sounded a shade too polished, and his hair looked so perfectly arranged.

If only he were taller, with untamed hair and a midnight-dark voice, she'd go to him, put her arms around him, ask him to . . . .

Bentley vaulted off the couch and rushed to the bar. She sloshed some brandy at a glass, spilling most of it. One gulp seared her throat like liquid fire, but it did clear her head a bit. "Sorry," she apologized to her astounded audience. "I was thinking about something else."

She couldn't explain that she'd seen a mirage, that for a fleeting second, Reid had stood within her reach. They'd call the men in white coats for sure.

Resurrecting the smile, she turned to ask her cousin a question that—hopefully—made sense. Her words were cut off, replaced by a soft moan. Merciful heaven, did they have to be so overt? Adrian's hand was spread over Beth's belly, rubbing their baby, smiling that sappy smile reserved for the blissfully happy. Bentley wanted to cry. She simply could not bear any more tangible reminders of what she had lost.

She slammed the glass to the bar and dashed to the door. "Mother, Bill, I have to leave. I need some time to myself." Seeing their distress, she added, "Don't worry. I'll be fine after I've had some rest." She escaped before anyone could try to change her mind.

"Oh, Bill," Victoria said shakily. "Nothing's working out as I'd hoped. Losing Reid is tearing her apart. What are we going to do?"

"Don't worry, Tori," he said, patting her arm. "Let's give her the time she says she needs. Then I'll have a talk with her. This foolishness has gone on long enough."

Bentley had collapsed across her bed the minute she arrived home, not bothering to remove her clothes or shoes. Several hours later she awoke stiff-necked and groggy, with the promise of a headache lurking behind her eyes.

And she'd had the dream again.

She fumbled her way to the bathroom before flipping on a light. After splashing water on her face, she took two aspirin and brushed her teeth. A hot shower would do wonders for her aching neck, but it required more effort than she cared to exert. So she slipped on a soft cotton gown and went back to the bedroom. Just as she reached for the light, the doorbell rang.

Bentley knew it would be Victoria or Bill, or both. She'd expected them sooner. At least now she was more rational and in control. She could assure them that all she needed was sleep and send them home with a promise to come by first thing in the morning. They were both dear, but sometimes they fussed too much.

She threw open the door without looking through the viewer or using the intercom.

"I couldn't stay away any longer."

His deep, raspy confession set off a flare of heat deep inside her. She was powerless to close the door and shut him out of her life. She couldn't even speak.

"I tried. But the . . . emptiness . . . it just kept getting worse till I couldn't stand it."

"Yes." How well she understood the emptiness, a great black void that nothing could fill.

"Finally tonight, I had to come."

"Yes," she said again, and stood aside to admit him, locking the door with a final-sounding click.

"You're not going to turn me away."

Not yet. She wasn't that strong. "No."

Reid brought their lips together with lightning speed and fearsome power, releasing a torrent of long-denied passion. Mouths open, tongues seeking, he drew in her breath, she returned his moan, and they were lost.

His hands moved up her arms, over her shoulders, down her spine to grasp the backs of her thighs. He lifted her, cradled her against the bold confirmation of his desire, moving sinuously while his tongue worked magic on her ear.

"Aaah, Reid," she whispered, straining to absorb all of him, frustrated by the clothing that prevented her from taking him completely into her.

"I need you. Let me love you."

Bentley hesitated, a small remnant of logic warning her to send him away before it was too late. "Reid, I don't—"

"Hush." He silenced her mouth with his own, a kiss full of passion and love.

Bentley never gave up responsibility for her actions, never did anything without weighing the consequences. Tonight was no exception. She knew what this would cost, and she was willing to pay the price.

They had no future, but his being here offered her a moment out of time. A treasure to be hoarded for those interminable nights when she would need Reid but couldn't have him.

"I want you," she murmured on a thread of sound.

He swept her into his arms and strode to the bed. As if possessed, they fought with each other's clothing, tore at their own until there was nothing to feel but bare, fevered flesh.

"I can't wait." They said the words simultaneously as their bodies sought, found, joined. Their coming together was wild and sudden, the explosion swift and cataclysmic, the aftermath shockingly silent.

Reid rolled away and sat on the edge of the bed. As if unsure of what to do, he drew the cool satin comforter over Bentley, gently tucking it around her.

"Bentley?" he said unsteadily. "Honey, I'm sorry. I had no right to take you like that. So rough. So fast."

The skin along his shoulders and across his back was stretched taut as a drumhead. Bentley reached to touch it, to alleviate his guilt. "Reid, please don't say anything more. It happened. It's history. Our feelings took over, and we let them. It's what we both wanted and needed."

He turned, searching for what had been left unsaid.

"And now, you have to go." Even under the heavy quilt, Bentley was beginning to shiver.

"No, I can't. Don't you see, we're meant to—"

"Don't *you* see? Nothing has changed. You're still who you are and I am fighting to prove myself equal to you. That's what separates us, what will always keep us apart."

"I can't accept that," he said woodenly, staring down at his balled fists.

Bentley leaned against the headboard, propped up by two pillows. "I know you're determined, I know you're tenacious." She sighed, almost too tired to speak. "But this time, I have to be more so."

"What are you saying?"

"I guess the simplest way to put it is good-bye."

"I refuse to give up, Bentley. I fight for what I want. And I get it. Look at the record."

"I know," she said softly. "Reid Hunter always wins. But there's a first time for everything. Maybe it's your turn to lose." Bentley's feelings and emotions rode too close to the surface, as they had so often since she'd known him. She willed the moisture filling her eyes not to become tears.

"How can you let go of something this good?"

She steeled herself not to respond to the agony in his voice. This was all his fault. How dare he try to make it sound like her mistake? "It's easy to let go," she flung back. "All I have to do is remind myself that you're very methodically ruining my stepfather."

Something dangerous flared in his eyes, but Bentley was beyond caution. She wanted to wound and punish, to make him hurt more than she did.

"Bentley I give you my word Bill Rutledge will not be ruined. I'll see to that."

She felt a drop escape her eye and roll down her cheek. "Reid, just go. I don't want to hear any more."

"I'm afraid you have no choice."

"I remember telling you months ago that I'd never begged for anything, that I wouldn't know how." Her words sounded dim, distant, like the eerie half-light from the adjoining room. "Well, I'm begging you now. Please don't try to see me or talk to me. Please, please leave me alone."

"I don't think I can," he said earnestly. "I need you too much."

"I asked you for something once, and you said it was impossible. That even if you'd wanted to, you couldn't do it." He tried to interrupt her, but she forced the protest back in his mouth. "It is in your power to do this for me, and I'm begging. I never want to see you again."

Reid heard the condemning words and his natural inclination was to argue, to make her back down. But he knew neither of them was in any condition to prolong this. He felt hollow, strung out, in no shape to reassure her that he would take care of everything. He wasn't so sure he had all the answers anyway.

He leaned over to sift through the pile of tangled clothes strewn alongside the bed. Using every bit of energy he could muster, he put on his slacks and shoes.

His shirt was under Bentley's gown, and for some reason, pulling it out hurt like a knifeblade in the heart.

Rising slowly, he buttoned his shirt while looking down at her. "You're the only thing I ever really wanted that I was afraid I'd never have." He bent to retrieve his leather windbreaker before turning back to her.

"All my life . . . it's almost as if I've been charmed. I know what I want, and somehow I know how to go about getting it." He pressed his leg against the edge of the bed, as if it could substitute for touching her. "But with you . . . hell, I screwed up with my very first words. And I never quite figured out how to make it right."

"You made it very right for a while. I don't ever expect to find anything so right again."

The knifeblade moved to his throat. For a long time, Reid couldn't speak. He made himself go on. This might be his last chance.

"Do you know what haunts someone who's gotten everything he wanted?" Her eyes were wide, brimming, and she shook her head. "It's that hidden fear eating at you, taunting that someday you'll want something really bad, more than you've ever wanted anything. But you won't be able to get it. You'll have used up your quota of luck on a bunch of useless crap that means absolutely nothing."

"I'm sorry," she said, dabbing her eyes with the sheet. "Sorry it has to end like this, sorry for both of us."

Reid nodded, a lifetime of fatigue suddenly bearing down on him. "I love you, Bentley." He touched her damp cheek with the back of his hand. "I've never said that to another woman. You have my promise that I never will.''

Reid found himself sitting in the Porsche, in his usual parking spot without knowing how he'd gotten there. Instinct, he supposed. Just as instinct drew him to his office. How many nights had he spent here by himself in this building? Hundreds. But never before had he felt so aimless and devoid of purpose.

He couldn't recall a time when he'd felt this tired or weak, a bone-deep exhaustion so invasive that if he gave in to it and lay down, he might never be able to get up again.

He braced his hip against the desk and picked up Bentley's scarf, the one that had fluttered into his hand when she ran from his office. It was bright and vivid, like the woman herself. He drew it through his fingers, rubbing the silk, remembering the texture of her skin.

A prickle of awareness coursed through him. He could almost feel her skin coming alive under his touch, feel her hands stroking him, making him come alive, too.

He'd waited so long for her, had held her so fleetingly. How could he give her up? He drifted over to the window, staring out at the deserted grounds of Maverick. This had been his life for eight years, and he'd devoted all his time and energy to it.

Without looking at it, Reid twirled an antique globe on its axis. He often spun the globe while he mulled over business decisions. It helped focus his thoughts. He smiled bitterly. Like a fool, he'd been guilty of believing the world was his.

A storm front was moving in from the north. Wind gusts rattled the glass panes in the old building and he could see palm fronds whipping furiously in the gale. One sturdy tree stood apart from a cluster of others, alone, fighting its battle independently. Just as Reid had done all his life.

He'd always been an anomaly, a dreamer *and* a doer. He'd never been much of a team player, much to the disgust of his father, The Coach. His dreams were solitary, and he made them reality by himself.

Then he had met Bentley and suddenly he lived in a new world. After so long he'd found a woman he wanted to share everything with—ideas, plans, goals. He wanted to work with her, live with her, love her. She filled the empty spaces he hadn't known about, made him realize he hadn't known what complete happiness was.

But tonight she had begged him to never see her again.

Reid wanted her to be happy, but she was asking too much of him. He wasn't strong enough without her. It was a sobering lesson to learn that he wasn't hard and tough and invincible after all. He was lonely and desolate and defeated.

He dropped into his chair and gazed out over the neat, polished surface of his desk. Nearly everything he'd accomplished had begun right here. Now he felt as if it were all ending here.

Reid thought about all he'd wanted and all he'd gotten. He thought about all he'd lost. He rubbed the scarf over his cheek, heard it rasp against the stubble of his beard. He buried his face in the silk and drew in a ragged breath. Her perfume lingered. . . .

"Oh, God," he moaned, shaking his head. It wasn't the scarf. Her perfume was on *him*, all over him, a reminder of their loving.

In despair, he spread his arms on the desk, resting his head on them. And for the first time since he was eight years old, Reid Hunter wept.

The aging black Cadillac was coasting to a stop in front of Bentley's townhouse when Bill saw Reid Hunter come out the door and walk to his sports car. Hunter's hands were in his pockets, his head was bowed, his shoulders slumped. He looked like a disheartened man.

Bill let his engine idle, thinking while he waited for the Porsche to leave. He'd come to see Bentley, but was struck by a better idea. When the other car finally pulled away, he followed it.

He fumbled in his pocket for a cigar and tore at the wrapping. Once he had it in his mouth he had to fight a strong temptation to fire it up. He resisted. The only time he allowed himself the pleasure was when he had something special to celebrate. He wasn't in that position yet, but a plan was forming.

Would he be able to sell it to Bentley? She was so intelligent and capable and independent, he thought proudly. So determined to carry the torch. But she was hurting. Couldn't a father be forgiven for meddling if it protected his little girl from pain?

Bill was a half block behind when the Porsche pulled into a parking spot at Maverick headquarters. By the time he'd stopped the Cadillac, Hunter was already inside one of the buildings. Bill waited a few minutes, contemplating how to approach the man . . . the man Bentley loved. When he was sure he had his thoughts organized, he struck out.

Just as he was about to enter the president's office, he heard the sound. He couldn't believe his ears. His brow knit, his head tipped to one side, and he peered around the doorfacing.

When he saw Reid, Bill clawed at the wall for support and chomped down on his cigar hard enough to bite through it. For a long time he stood dumbstruck, inhaling deeply. Then he heard a fist connect with wood and one very determined avowal, and he quietly backtracked to his car.

First thing in the morning, he'd talk to Bentley and get all this nonsense ironed out. The scene he had inadvertently witnessed tonight would go to his grave with him, forever a secret between the two men who loved Bentley, each in his own way.

But any man who could cry over the loss of a woman might go to just about any lengths to get her back.

Once inside his car, he very deliberately pushed in the cigarette lighter and waited in anticipation. What if Tori had been right all along? Maybe love *could* transcend everything and be the great healer.

THIRTEEN

Bentley sailed into the Rutledges' dining room early the next morning. "I have to talk to you," she said, waving off Bill's offer of breakfast. The previous night had been long, and she hadn't closed her eyes, but she *had* faced reality head-on. Today she had to act on her conclusions.

"What's on your mind, hon?" Bill asked before chomping into a toasted English muffin.

"I have a confession to make." Bentley pulled out one of the side chairs and sat very straight in it. "I've been letting my involvement with Reid color my judgment where Willco's best interests are concerned."

"What do you mean?" Bill stopped eating and eyed her with interest.

"Just that I was hurt personally by Reid and I guess I saw fighting him as a means of retaliation." She picked up a knife from her mother's place setting, studying the ornate Grand Baroque pattern. "I thought it would make me feel better, but it hasn't. And it hasn't helped Willco."

Bill pushed his chair back, angling it to face her. "What exactly are you saying, B.B.?"

"I've researched everything I could find about take-overs, and talked to a lot of people who've seen them from both sides. The consensus seems to be that, in most instances, the company would have been better off with the original raider than with its rescuer."

Bill nodded. "I've heard that, too."

"And with the oil business being iffy at best, it would be suicidal to spend the money on a buy back. The debt load would be staggering."

Bentley carefully replaced the knife and looked Bill in the eye. "Our best shot at salvaging anything worthwhile is to meet with Hunter and see if we can talk them into some concessions. I'll do the best job of negotiating that I can." She got to her feet and went to her stepfather, patting him lightly on the shoulder.

"Bill, it pains me to disappoint you this way. But I don't know what else to do. I understand that this is a terrible blow to you and I'm sorry I can't preserve Willco as it's always been, the company you built."

"Sit down. I have a confession to make, too." He reached into the breast pocket of his western-cut suit and extracted a cigar wrapped in plain cellophane. He rolled it between his thumb and index finger, but didn't unwrap it. "B.B., I'm tired."

Bentley took the chair nearest him, sensing that he was finally going to explain why he'd remained so oddly detached from the takeover. "Maybe all you need is some time off, a chance to relax." She recalled the day Reid had prescribed the same thing for them.

"Funny, but your mother's been pestering me to do the same thing. For several years now. She wants to travel, get away from Houston in the summer. Fancies a place in the mountains around Telluride." Slowly, methodically, he peeled back the cellophane, as if he were going to find a surprise inside and wanted to prolong the suspense.

"I think it would be wonderful if the two of you spent more time together." Bentley smiled at the ecstatic look on Bill's face when he sniffed the cigar. "You've always worked too hard."

"I had to work hard. At least from the time I was fourteen years old. It got to be a habit. Then when it started paying off, it was easy to keep going." The cigar breached his lips. "But it isn't as much fun as it used to be. Hasn't been for a long time."

"Are you saying you *want* to get out of the oil business?" Unsure of how such a decision might affect her, Bentley didn't know whether to wail or cheer.

"Don't suppose I'll ever get completely out of it. Oil seeps into your blood." Bill evaluated the cigar and nodded. "But I'd sure as hell like to let somebody else fight the battles on a day-to-day basis."

Bentley felt herself wilting. If he was serious about semiretiring, did he expect her to step in? She forced herself to ask, "Do you have someone else in mind? To fight the daily battles?"

"Well, dang it, Hunter's a damned good businessman. Plus he's got . . . brass. He's the type to ride out the rough times and make Willco better in the good. Could be the company needs his young blood."

When he saw the shocked look on Bentley's face, he smiled. "B.B., I always liked the idea that your children would be running Willco on down the road. If I thought you wanted to take it over in the meantime,

I'd hold on with both hands. But you don't. Hell, girl, I may be old, but I ain't blind.''

Bentley laughed for the first time in days. Bill was even shrewder than she'd given him credit for. "Are you serious? I mean about letting Reid take us over?''

Bill's smile was decidedly smug. "You can usually tell the caliber of a man by measuring the amount of opposition it takes to discourage him.'' His smile spread even broader. "I'm not sure there's any force on earth that can discourage Reid Hunter.'' With that pronouncement, he whipped out a match and lighted the forbidden cigar with bravado.

Bentley was staring speechless when her mother breezed into the room. Victoria noted the cigar, but refrained from criticizing it or Bill. "Bentley dear, Reid's on the phone.''

"What did I tell you?'' Bill said, expelling a giant puff of smoke as Bentley rose to answer the summons. "Oh, and B.B.,'' he said to her departing back, "tell him his cigars are damned good.''

Bentley paused outside the door of Reid's office. How many times in the past seven months had she stood here, dreading, anticipating, arming herself for what awaited her inside? Today was the most important, by far.

She'd had three days since the early-morning phone call from Reid, three days to draft terms for a friendly takeover of Willco by Reid's partnership. Bentley's first decision had been to approach him as if she were negotiating from a position of strength rather than from her relatively powerless state.

She didn't have any illusions that Reid would be

fooled, but talking tough would fuel her confidence, a factor she had to be always mindful of around him.

One thing she knew—you didn't get anything unless you asked for it, and asked for it in a way that conveyed you expected to get it.

Bentley glanced at her watch. Right on time. She adjusted the high neck of her starched cotton blouse and smoothed the dark navy skirt of her tailored wool suit. Today it was essential that she come off as a competent businesswoman with no hint of softness. She rapped on the door and entered.

"Ms. North."

Déjà vu. She watched his eyes flick over her, the intimacy belying his formal greeting. Then a transitory smile lifted his lips as he took in the clothes. When his gaze riveted on the ring, the smile became permanent, predatory. Bentley uttered a silent curse. After rehearsing every move so precisely, how could she have committed a major tactical blunder like wearing his emerald?

She'd tried returning the ring with no message, only to have it redelivered with very concise orders. "This is yours. Unless you want a headline-making scene, keep it!"

Bentley had begun wearing the exquisite stone after that, telling herself it would be a crime to lock it away in a bank vault. She'd never admit that its constant presence on her hand comforted her, gave her a little bit of Reid.

But she ought to have taken it off for this meeting. "Mr. Hunter." She chose the same chair she'd sat in for her first interview. "I know you're busy, and that Willco has been pending for weeks. Let's not waste any more time."

His head dipped once, then he leaned it back and observed her through slitted eyelids. "Start with what you want."

It was disconcerting that, with so few words, he could take the offensive and put himself in control. It had always been like this. Certain that dragging it out wouldn't make it easier, Bentley plunged in, delivering all her demands at once, like a well-memorized speech.

He listened, his expression blank, while she asked that Bill and three other directors remain on the board, that neither staff nor Willco's budget for exploration would be cut for at least a year and that for the rest of his life, Bill be provided an office in corporate headquarters. She followed with a string of lesser demands, included to allow her some flexibility in dealing.

When she finished, slightly breathless, he continued to look at her. Knowing it was unprofessional, Bentley moved her fingers from his line of sight and crossed them.

At last, he said, "All right."

She almost fell out of her chair. She must not have heard correctly. "What did you say?"

"I said, 'all right.' That I don't have serious problems with any of those requirements. We'll probably have to do some dickering on the matter of staff, but I imagine we can work out the details to our mutual satisfaction."

"You do?" The squeak in her voice revealed that she hadn't been as confident as she'd tried to sound.

"Yeah." He apparently found her astonishment amusing. "What's the matter, North? Can't you accept victory gracefully?"

"Victory?" She supposed in a way it was. "Yes, of

course I can. It's just that I—'' What was nagging her? He'd agreed to more than she'd imagined possible. So why wasn't she turning cartwheels and reveling in her triumph? Bentley concentrated on the emerald's fire, and the answer came to her. Too clearly.

The victory had been too easy. A tough maverick like Reid Hunter did not roll over and play dead at the bargaining table. As a matter of principle, he wouldn't grant anyone's demands without making even more of his own.

"What do you want?" Every cell in her body vibrated with the knowledge that his reply would mean personal disaster for her.

"For starters, you back at Maverick."

Of all the things he could have asked, why must it be this? "That's impossible."

"It's not negotiable."

She could see from the implacable set of his features that it wasn't. He had her trapped and they both knew it. If she refused, Bill and Willco would be at his mercy, and she doubted that he would be feeling merciful toward them.

Working so close to him, and yet being so far apart, would be torture. She'd been resolute about not seeing him again, but that didn't diminish her feelings for him. She had hoped that time would enable her to get over him. Working at Maverick made that unlikely. Bentley didn't trust herself when Reid was near.

He spoke, as if reading her mind. "What's the problem?" He sat forward in his chair. "I gave you everything you wanted, and I'm not asking for much in return. Just you back in my legal department, back in my bed, back in my future."

Bentley gasped, appalled. "Surely you don't expect

that we can take up where we left off before all this."
She gestured at the notes on his desk.

"That's exactly what I expect. I asked you to marry
me and you consented. As far as I'm concerned, that
hasn't changed."

"How can you think that?" she asked incredulously.
"Things may not have changed in your opinion, but let
me assure you the situation appears quite different from
my perspective." She had hoped they could steer clear
of personal issues in this meeting.

"Bentley," he said with forced patience, "we've re-
solved the business differences. Why shouldn't we resume our relationship? My feelings for you are the
same. Stronger, in fact." His eyes slid over her like
a torch. "And after the other night in your bedroom, I
think you want me just as much."

Short of lying, she couldn't deny it, so she looked
away. "Feelings won't enter into any discussion between us now or in the future. Don't try to force the
issue."

"Why are you doing this to us?" He stood, stuffing
his hands into his pockets. "If you want an apology,
okay. I'm sorry it happened. It isn't the end of the
world, though."

"Why can't you understand that whatever we had
together is over? I've spelled out why several times."

"I can't understand because it makes no sense.
You're just trying to punish me. I won't put up with
games like this, Bentley," he said, his rumbling voice
taking on an intimidating element.

Did he honestly think this was a game to her? "I'll
make it as plain as I can, Reid. There is no hope for
us because I'll never be able to trust you completely
again. I can't forget what you did, and that, in the final

analysis, you didn't love me enough to even try to stop the takeover.''

He sucked in a breath, as if she'd slugged him. "That's a vicious accusation, one that's pretty damned hard to fight."

"Then don't try. Let it go. I will agree to come back to Maverick . . . if you insist. But I need time first."

He scowled and she could almost see his temper heating up. "How much time?"

"Two weeks. During which you have to leave me alone. Don't try to contact me at all. After that, I will be an employee, nothing more."

He considered her terms during a long silence, then nodded once. "If that's how it has to be."

"It does. And *that's* not negotiable." Bentley made a fast exit before he could tack on any amendments. She'd already made the supreme sacrifice.

Reid watched the door close behind Bentley and felt his hunter's instinct come to life. One corner of his mouth quirked. "I thought you knew, North. *Everything's* negotiable."

Bentley took her first relaxed breath in weeks when the Jag crossed the bridge spanning Copano Bay. As she covered the last six miles into Rockport, she grew increasingly calm. She had fallen in love with the little town during the time she'd spent remodeling Reid's beach house. It seemed the logical place to pick for a recovery getaway.

She needed to escape Houston until she could regain her equilibrium. Bentley didn't delude herself that going back to Maverick would be easy, but she was determined to see it through. Once her strength and self-confidence regenerated, she could master anything.

Oddly enough, she didn't find it incongruous to have chosen Reid's house as her hideout. Though his name was on the deed, he'd never seen the place. It was her project start to finish and she felt possessive of the results. He'd never even asked her to return the keys.

She drove past a familiar grove of live oaks, bent leeward by the Gulf breeze, and slowed for the series of curves that led to Key Allegro beach. Once on Bayshore, the roadway straightened and she sped up, anxious to be there.

Her tires crunched to a halt on the oyster-shell drive and Bentley shut off the engine. Opening her door so she could inhale the ocean scent, she sat quietly for a long time. Then she climbed the streetside steps up to a gate which opened onto the deck. She dumped her bags at the main entrance and continued on around to gaze out over the water.

There was no beach left—the latest hurricane had claimed it—and now, at high tide, the Gulf washed relentlessly against the house's deeply anchored pilings.

Bentley felt the inexorable ebb and flow beneath her, and knew that here she would find the answers she sought. One way or another, when she went back, she'd do so with her future mapped out. Like the gradual advance of the sea, life had to go forward.

Three days later, Bentley had worked halfway through a shopping bag of novels. Her routine never varied. She rose early and ate a light breakfast. It was warm for November, and by ten she could put on a bathing suit and spend the remainder of the day on the deck, absorbing the gentle sun.

Inevitably, Reid occupied her thoughts. She loved

him, and as she saw it, there were two courses of action open to her. She could be a martyr to a dead cause and be forever miserable, or she could act like a woman in love. Meaning, she could accept that Reid made mistakes like everyone else and deserved to be forgiven for them.

In retrospect, Bentley saw that perhaps she'd judged him too harshly, expected too much of him. She didn't need him to be perfect; she only needed him to love her. He had sworn he did, and if there was one certainty in this world, it was that Reid didn't lie.

When she got back to Houston, she'd go to him, tell him about her decision, and ask if they could start over. Perhaps in slow, building increments, they could recapture the closeness and respect they'd once shared.

The first week passed, each day comforting in its sameness. Around five she would shower and go out for an early dinner. Even after dark, she needed the freedom of outdoors so every night she donned a jacket and sat out on the deck. The surf sounds lulled her into such a tranquil state that her dreams were restful and happy.

At this time of year, few people were in residence on Bayshore. But during the second week, Bentley noticed someone on the deck directly across from Reid's. Each night when she came out, the shadowy outline intrigued her, tantalized and lured her. . . .

For four consecutive nights she watched him—size proclaimed him male—across the dark expanse. She felt an inexplicable affinity for the stranger whom she saw no sign of in the light of day. A profound communion arced between them like an intangible bond.

Tonight she was especially attuned to him. He seemed closer, almost touchable. She knew he smoked, and for some reason didn't find it objectionable. Now she could identify it as a cigar, the aroma curiously familiar as it drifted to her on the breeze.

That night when she slept, the dream had more definition. Reid didn't appear as a misty illusion; he came directly to her from across the way, gliding over the sand that separated the decks.

Bentley wrenched herself awake, positive of the compelling stranger's identity. No wonder she'd been so drawn to him. It was no stranger at all. It was Reid!

In typical Hunter fashion, he hadn't been able to wait for something to happen. He'd had to take action. Bentley smiled as a devious plan took shape. She'd show him action.

Reid paced like a temperamental lion through the four rooms of his friend Jack's beach house. Every few circuits he peered out a small opening in the blinds, but there was no sign of Bentley's car. Had she gone home? He didn't think so. He'd watched her leave shortly before ten and she hadn't taken any luggage.

Lord, he was acting like some sleazy gumshoe, sneaking in here at two o'clock in the morning, holing up for days, peeking through cracks. All because of Bentley.

She'd told him not to contact her for two weeks, and he hadn't tried. But after the first week, he'd been such a basket case that Marian had shooed him out of his own office. "You're driving everybody nuts," she'd said.

Things had really gotten critical when he didn't have the pretense of work. It was then that he decided he had to find Bentley. He wasn't sure how he knew where she would be, but somehow he did. He'd told himself he just wanted to make sure she was all right, that he wouldn't bother her. Which was why he'd borrowed Jack's place.

But after four days of watching her do the same things, he was itching to get out of the house. He didn't dare. She might return any minute and he'd have a tough time explaining why he was bird-dogging her.

In fact, he'd done much more than spy. He had come to some conclusions. He and Bentley were going to be together, no matter how long he had to hammer away at her to get it.

Late that afternoon, he heard her car. He watched as she made several trips between her Jag and the house, arms loaded with packages. "Damn!" Just like a woman. She'd gone shopping while he'd been left chewing nails.

He squinted, trying to see what all her activity was about. He could detect movement, but couldn't tell precisely what she was doing. When it began to get dark, she turned on some lights without drawing the vertical blinds closed. Good. Now maybe he could tell what was going on.

She vanished into what he assumed was a bedroom and didn't come out for nearly an hour. It was now quite dark and Reid could clearly see that she wore something long and flowing. It looked silky, clinging to her breasts and swirling around her hips and legs when she walked.

He watched her place a large flower arrangement on a table in front of the window, and a distressing thought took hold. Reid let out a menacing snarl and started to rummage through closets and cabinets. His frantic search finally turned up a pair of binoculars.

"Jeez, this is ridiculous." But he opened the blinds

fully and focused the lens. It was pretty bad when he had to get the first glimpse of his own house through binoculars. The interior looked cool, clean, and comfortable. He'd known Bentley would do the job right.

The glasses were trained on what appeared to be a combination living and dining area. The walls were pale aqua, the floor stark white, and the furniture a combination of the two with scattered touches of yellow. He liked what he could see of his house. But he didn't like what he saw happening inside it.

"I don't believe this," he seethed. Bentley was getting ready to entertain company for dinner. And not just company—a man. He could tell. Why else would she be wearing that slinky caftan thing that matched the twin sofas? Or fussing with the huge bowl of flowers?

"What the hell?" She'd just carried a wine cooler to the white iron-and-glass table and was putting a bottle of champagne in it. When she lighted candles and dimmed the lights, then walked to the door as if she expected someone momentarily, Reid slammed down the binoculars and scrambled for the doorknob.

Bentley smiled as she saw the shadow approach. He was shortening the distance with fast, determined strides. Her ploy had worked. Reid wrenched open the heavy sliding door and she jumped back in mock surprise.

"Reid, what are you doing here? I thought—"

"What did you think, Bentley? That you could stage a seduction right here—*in my house*—and get away with it?" Outrage poured from him in waves.

"I didn't—"

"Did you imagine that I'd finish the house in the Heights just for you and let some other man have you in this one?"

"It's not—"

"Did you believe that when I found the woman I want to spend the rest of my life with, the one I want to be equal partners with in every way, I'd ever let anyone else touch you?" He loomed over her, a towering specimen of affronted male. "Well, Bentley, did you?"

"No, of course I didn't." His body pulsated with indignation and she touched him gently. "Why don't you calm down and open the champagne?"

He raised one brow, eyes shifting between her and the wine cooler on the table. At last he moved to lift a bottle of Dom Pérignon out of the bucket.

"Hmmph," he grunted, but Bentley saw the dawning realization spread over his face when he recognized the brand they had ordered to toast their engagement.

His mustache twitched though his tone was serious. "Mind telling me what you're planning to cook for this little party?"

"Why, hazelnut steak, naturally. It's what I always insist on when I celebrate. Remember?"

"Oh, yeah," he said in a dark, husky voice. They both waited. The air between them crackled with tension, with promise. "Don't torture me any longer. What are we celebrating?"

Though he stood still she felt him reach out to her. "That I love you, Reid."

He moved so quickly that he swallowed his name off her lips; at the same time he wrapped her in an embrace that might have crushed her had she not needed it so desperately.

"Bentley! God, honey. I love you, too." It took him a long time to get the words out because he couldn't stop kissing her. "I have so much to tell you—"

"Later," she whispered. "We have forever." She sealed the pledge with her lips.

He withdrew, but only far enough to ask, "How did you know it was me over there?"

Bentley smiled at him, the full measure of her love shining in her eyes. "Because you're my dream come true."

SHARE THE FUN . . .
SHARE YOUR NEW-FOUND TREASURE!!

You don't want to let your new books out of your sight?
That's okay. Your friends can get their own. Order below.

No. 23 A PERFECT MATCH by Susan Combs
Ross can keep Emily safe but can he save himself from Emily?

No. 24 REMEMBER MY LOVE by Pamela Macaluso
Will Max ever remember the special love he and Deanna shared?

No. 25 LOVE WITH INTEREST by Darcy Rice
Stephanie & Elliot find $47,000,000 *plus* interest—true love!

No. 26 NEVER A BRIDE by Leanne Banks
The last thing Cassie wanted was a relationship. Joshua had other ideas.

No. 27 GOLDILOCKS by Judy Christenberry
David and Susan join forces and get tangled in their own web.

No. 28 SEASON OF THE HEART by Ann Hammond
Can Lane and Maggie's newfound feelings stand the test of time?

No. 29 FOSTER LOVE by Janis Reams Hudson
Morgan comes home to claim his children but Sarah claims his heart.

No. 30 REMEMBER THE NIGHT by Sally Falcon
Joanna throws caution to the wind. Is Nathan fantasy or reality?

No. 31 WINGS OF LOVE by Linda Windsor
Mac & Kelly soar to new heights of ecstasy. Are they ready?

No. 32 SWEET LAND OF LIBERTY by Ellen Kelly
Brock has a secret and Liberty's freedom could be in serious jeopardy!

No. 33 A TOUCH OF LOVE by Patricia Hagan
Kelly seeks peace and quiet and finds paradise in Mike's arms.

No. 34 NO EASY TASK by Chloe Summers
Hunter is wary when Doone delivers a package that will change his life.

No. 35 DIAMOND ON ICE by Lacey Dancer
Diana could melt even the coldest of hearts. Jason hasn't a chance.

No. 36 DADDY'S GIRL by Janice Kaiser
Slade wants more than Andrea is willing to give. Who wins?

No. 37 ROSES by Caitlin Randall
It's an inside job & K.C. helps Brett find more than the thief!

No. 38 HEARTS COLLIDE by Ann Patrick
Matthew finds big trouble and it's spelled P-a-u-l-a.

No. 39 QUINN'S INHERITANCE by Judi Lind
Gabe and Quinn share an inheritance and find an even greater fortune.

No. 40 CATCH A RISING STAR by Laura Phillips
Justin is seeking fame; Beth helps him find something more important.

No. 41 SPIDER'S WEB by Allie Jordan
Silvia's quiet life explodes when Fletcher shows up on her doorstep.

No. 42 TRUE COLORS by Dixie DuBois
Julian helps Nikki find herself again but will she have room for him?

No. 43 DUET by Patricia Collinge
Adam & Marina fit together like two perfect parts of a puzzle!

No. 44 DEADLY COINCIDENCE by Denise Richards
J.D.'s instincts tell him he's not wrong; Laurie's heart says trust him.

No. 45 PERSONAL BEST by Margaret Watson
Nick is a cynic; Tess, an optimist. Where does love fit in?

No. 46 ONE ON ONE by JoAnn Barbour
Vincent's no saint but Loie's attracted to the devil in him anyway.

Meteor Publishing Corporation
Dept. 492, P. O. Box 41820, Philadelphia, PA 19101-9828

Please send the books I've indicated below. Check or money order only—no cash, stamps or C.O.D.s (PA residents, add 6% sales tax). I am enclosing $2.95 plus 75¢ handling fee for *each* book ordered.

Total Amount Enclosed: $_____.

____ No. 23	____ No. 29	____ No. 35	____ No. 41
____ No. 24	____ No. 30	____ No. 36	____ No. 42
____ No. 25	____ No. 31	____ No. 37	____ No. 43
____ No. 26	____ No. 32	____ No. 38	____ No. 44
____ No. 27	____ No. 33	____ No. 39	____ No. 45
____ No. 28	____ No. 34	____ No. 40	____ No. 46

Please Print:
Name _____
Address _____ Apt. No. _____
City/State _____ Zip _____

Allow four to six weeks for delivery. Quantities limited.